Vindictive Wo-Men
By
Valencia R. Williams

Vindictive Wo-Men (Women/Men)

Jones and Williams Publication, LLC

P. O. Box 210460

Auburn, MI 48321-0406

E-mail: joneswilliamspublishing@yahoo.com

Bookworld Distributor 1-888-444-2524 EXT 505

Written

by

VALENCIA RENAY WILLIAMS

Cover Design by Legwork/NULookMagazine/313.779.4225

Editing by Donna L. Lopez-exhortations.literary@yahoo.com

Second Printing January 2006

ISBN 0-9740132-5-0

Printed in the United States of America

Book also written by this author
"The Hottest Summer Ever Known"

Wo-Men
Represents
Women and Men

In the loving memory of my Dad,
Gilbert Williams, Sr.
I miss you

You may now proceed
at your own risk......

Foolish Love

"A young mind that's not fully developed, could be the one that lead you to a grave"

Jamie Davis

There were no words that could define Jamie Davis. This young diva had what many young teens her age dreamed of; parents that showered her with love, and friends that worshiped the ground she walked on.

So what went wrong?

A *"Black American Princess"* that sported a crown whenever she stepped into a room filled with people. Life was grand. All the young girls in the neighborhood envied her caramel-coated skin; her petite flawless body, and her naturally extended hair, which she closely maintained at her father's expense.

Jamie was a natural born threat to any man that laid eyes on her. Men found her age hard to believe. Jamie had the body and personality of a 25 year-old woman. Standing at 5'9, complimented with nice firm breasts, the girl had it going on.

Who would have ever thought that *evil* could dwell inside of something so beautiful?

One thing Jamie held on to was her virginity. And even though her parents truly believed she was not having sex, they were still particular about the company she kept. They would go to the extreme, drawing a line to how far she could step away from their home without permission. All in all, those rules were soon to change.

One hot sunny day, Jamie and her girls were hanging out on the block when a Trans-Am designed like a racecar came roaring up the street. Jamie stopped what she was doing, placed her hands on her hips, and gave an evil stare at the midnight blue vehicle. She cursed the person driving all the way up the street until they reached their destination.

Jamie said to her girls, "Why does it always have to be a black ignorant muthafreaka that's got to show off his ride by speeding down the street playing that loud, obnoxious, rap music? He could have hit a little kid or something..."

They all went back and forth trying to make sense of the speed demon's stupidity.

They stood at the sidewalk waiting for this unknown, 'black ignorant fool' to exit the vehicle. To their surprise, the guy wasn't what they had expected.

Kilpatrick Jackson, one of the neighborhood's most notorious young hustlers stepped out of that car looking fine as ever. Jamie and her girls were caught in a daze, watching him walk toward his boy, throwing him a brotherly handshake and hug. Rumors had it that Kilpatrick not only had all the money one could spend, he even had lots of women and several fancy cars.

Something about his character instantly attracted Jamie to him.

Could it have been the fact that he was eight years older than her? Or was it because she couldn't have him the way she wanted him?

Kilpatrick and his boys hung out, while Jamie came up with a plan to gain his attention.

They ended up throwing on some music. They started dancing around, laughing and making a scene that drew Kilpatrick and his crew to the corner of her street. Before it was over, he was standing a few feet away from the line Jamie's parents prohibited her to cross.

"How old are you lil' Mama?" Kilpatrick asked, staring at her from head to toe.

She was caught up in his admiration. She turned to look at her girls, but they had scattered like ants! They knew the consequences if their parents had seen them talking to a thug.

"How old do I look?" She answered a question with a question, feeling a little nervous.

"Too young for me to fall in love with."

"That's cute. Anyway, I'm 15. So I guess I won't be able to experience love no time soon, huh?"

Jamie glanced back at her house to see if her parents were anywhere around.

"I don't know. I guess we'll just have to see. Let me get up out of here before your old dude tries to shoot me in the head. Here's my number, call me. " He smiled, sending monstrous waves through her.

"Mm-hum."

As Kilpatrick walked away, she said to herself, *I'm going to make you love me.*

And the nightmare begins...

*****

Jamie took a long hot bath, dried off, threw on a t-shirt and made her way to her room. She stared at her phone, wanting to call him so bad, but she didn't want to seem eager or desperate, so she waited a few days...

*****

A few days had gone by....

"Yeah!" The voice answered deeply giving her chills.

"Is Kilpatrick home?"

"Who dis?"

"Jamie."

"Jamie? Where do I know you from?"

"I'm the one that lives down the block from your boy over here on Freeland."

"Oh, shit. Aight, I remember you, what's up?"

"Nothing really, just lay'n around, that's all."

"Can I come over?"

"What? Are you trying to get us both killed?"

"Where your peeps at?" Kilpatrick asked anxiously.

"Sleep," she replied.

"Sneak me in then."

Jamie thought about it. She wanted to see him so badly that her body started to ache for his presence. Plus she felt that if she had said "no", he would never talk to her again. So, she agreed.

"Okay, but don't park in front of my house."

"Girl, I got this."

Within seconds he was at her side door.

Jamie slipped into her robe and let him in. He was strikingly sexy, and he smelled so good. If it meant her virginity tonight, so be it!

"Nice bed," he commented, taking a seat on her queen sized sleigh bed. "You're spoiled aren't you?"

"Why you say that?" She sat at her desk, staring in amazement at the most wanted player in the hood.

"Looking at this room, I can tell."

"Well if it's that obvious, why would you ask?" She sucked her teeth.

Their eyes met for what seemed like forever.

"Come here. Sit next to me." Kilpatrick patted the spot where he wanted her to sit. Jamie was nervous, but she followed his demand.

"Do I make you nervous?" he asked.

"A little," she replied.

"Have you ever been with a man before?" He whispered in her ear gently biting it with his teeth.

"No," she whispered timidly.

Interesting. He thought to himself.

He began to massage her back to relax her before he made his next move.

Kilpatrick felt a little uncomfortable being that Jamie was so young, but she wouldn't have been his first and definitely not his last.

He moved toward her breasts and before she realized it, he had her captive.

No victims just volunteers, he silently said.

"Ssss ooooo…girl…you makin' my dick hard. You know what to do with this right here?"

He grabbed his flesh, blinding her with his diamond ring that was reflecting brightly off the dim light on her desk. Jamie closed her eyes savoring each stroke of his hand across her nipples trying to calm her nerves.

"Relax lil' Mama. I won't hurt you. Let me tell you what I want you to do," he whispered.

Jamie opened her eyes slightly and was infatuated by the finest man she had ever seen in her life. Kilpatrick looked so good to her in his white tee and denim jeans. His complexion, his eyes, and chiseled body made him resemble a Black prince with an aggressive sex appeal. Jamie was even more amazed at how his flesh was just as chocolate as his skin.

Kilpatrick directed her straight to his rock hard tower. Jamie didn't know what to do, but Kilpatrick was an excellent coach. He only wanted one thing that night and that was his flesh soaked by the sweetness of her saliva, and sheltered by the warmth of her mouth. He got off on feeding young tenders like Jamie his rock hard stallion. It was something about the way they looked with their mouth draped around the head of his dick. It turned him on and then turned them out. As badly as he wanted to have sex with them, he knew rape would follow close behind and that would have been curtains. Somewhere in his corrupt mind he told himself that getting head was not as risky.

After that night with Jamie, impressed by her performance, Kilpatrick started coming through on a regular basis for a period of three months. The same routine applied each time he would come; bring him through the side door, sneak him in, and slide him into her mouth, *whole,* like savored dessert. Jamie became obsessed with Kilpatrick to a point where she was begging him to have sex with her. As bad as he wanted to, Kilpatrick knew he couldn't take a risk. He would just put her off each time saying, "The next time, Jamie". His intention was to buy as much time as he could until something better came around, and then he would disappear…

Kilpatrick didn't realize how desperate Jamie was. Not to mention that her patience with him was wearing thin. There was only so much she could handle before it ended up fatal.

*****

Something up her sleeve...

The night Jamie had been waiting for finally rolled around. She was determined to have sex with him no matter what it took!

Kilpatrick came over expecting the usual routine, pulling out his flesh and waiting for her to assume the position.

Jamie had a surprise for him this time. She made sure it was dark and her pearl was greased thoroughly. Once he made himself comfortable, laying his head back on the pillow. She pulled her mouth away and immediately climbed on top of him. He tried to push her away, but she had claimed her spot, leaving him no room to move. It was extremely painful, this being the first time she had sex, but the satisfaction of finally achieving her goal, made it worth her while.

"We-we can't do...do this Jamie."
He tried to fight the feeling of her tight flesh wrapped around him, but he couldn't. He was overtaken by a feeling he had been fighting against since they've been in touch.

Kilpatrick was hers for the moment. She rode him slowly, gently holding his neck with one hand and gripping his hand that held her waist with the other. The feeling became so good to her that out of the blue, she moaned, "Aaaaahhhh...Oh my...Oh sss...I love you Kilpatrick..."

Those three words were like acid to his soul, but it wasn't enough to force him to leave at that very moment. Kilpatrick had to admit to himself that the feeling from her straddling his flesh was good, but after tonight, he knew he could never return.

Racing for the finish line...

It took 15 minutes for Jamie to cum for the first time. She thought she had found her "Knight in Shining Armor." Kilpatrick was not trying to cum inside of her.

Kilpatrick was the one that always practiced self-control. But now, trapped inside of Jamie's web, all of discipline he was usually so good at was only moments from being sucked away dry...

"I'm about to cum...get up!" he moaned, exerting very little effort to push her away.

"No." Jamie said, tightening her muscles, locking him inside of her, holding him hostage.

"Jamie, I'm not playing. You can get pregnant girl!" He held on to her waist trying to fight against the feeling of wanting to give into her. Jamie's straddling was making Kilpatrick weak to a point where he was pulling her against him instead of away from him.

He moaned out again, "No...ssss, come on now! We can't do this!"

Time was closing in and a decision had to be made. He wanted to cum bad!

"I told you, I'm not moving." She straddled up, moved faster, squeezed her walls tighter, moved up and down, and marked her territory! Jamie locked in on him so tightly their pubic hairs entangled. Once he was prepared to let go, she dropped herself deeper into him, wanting to feel his stream of warmth.

"Auuuhhh! SSSss! Nooo...."

He couldn't hold back and Jamie accepted his sperm like a thirsty lost civilian, in a desert, that had just found water. She leaned into him, kissing him to silence his moans. Without pulling out, they kissed for as long as he would allow. She could feel his softened flesh tremble.

"Whose shit is this?" She whispered, using a line he used prior to this engagement.

"I got to go." He rose up, using her sheet from her bed to wipe himself off and then left without saying goodbye.

The next day Jamie was drained, beat down, and sore. Her sheets were bloody, and she had to get herself together before anyone noticed. She tried reaching Kilpatrick. No response. She waited a few hours assuming he was busy. No response. The next day came. No response. The day after...no response. Kilpatrick was ghost. Jamie was falling to pieces. She thought something had happened to him.

A week had gone by and she still hadn't heard from him. Kilpatrick and his mom lived a few blocks away. Jamie decided to make a visit to his home after school. She didn't know what to expect, but either way, she had to make sure Kilpatrick was okay.

"Who are you?" An older woman, that Jamie assumed was his mother, rudely answered the door.

"I'm sorry to bother you Ma'am, but is Kilpatrick home?"

The woman looked at her like she had lost her mind, showing up at her front door for her son, unexpectedly.

"What do you want with my son?" She asked, adamantly. "And you never told me who you were."

"A friend."

Jamie felt uncomfortable at that point. She tried to hold up a front with the woman, but she was losing patience.

"Let me tell you something, little lady!

Kilpatrick does not have girls showing up at my door unannounced! Did he inform you that he has a girlfriend with a baby on the way?" she asked spitefully, standing in her doorway with her arms folded.

"No, I'm sorry, he didn't. Sorry to have bothered you." Jamie's heart dropped.

The lady slammed the door, without saying another word.

"She has to be lying! He wouldn't do this to me! YOU LYING BITCH!!" Jamie looked back at the house and screamed, storming off down the street.

Jamie lost it. Her parents couldn't figure out what was wrong with her. She had completely shut down.

Days later, Kilpatrick started to receive numerous crank calls. He knew who it was. There was a time when Jamie called late one night; listening to his voice on the other end and not saying a word. That's when he shocked her saying, "Jamie? I know it's you." Then a woman voice in the background said, "Who is this Jamie girl?" Jamie could tell they were in bed together. He hung up and Jamie cried herself to sleep.

Jamie was plotting almost 24 hours a day; contemplating what she was going to do to get her man back. In spite of the fact that there was no commitment on his part, she made it clear saying, "You may not go with me! But I go with you!"

Kilpatrick appeared down the street one afternoon to visit his boy. As soon as Jamie heard his engine on his Trans Am, she threw on her get-up and made her way up the block.

"Kilpatrick?"

"Oh God." he said to his boy, Austin.

"Maaaan, what the fuck did you do to that girl?"

"I ain't did shit to her dawg. You know how these young freaks are. You give 'em a little phone conversation, then the next thing you know, they spreadin' rumors saying you fucked 'em!"

They talked amongst each other as she closely approached them.

"What girl!" Kilpatrick snapped.

"What girl?" she retorted, confused by his tone.

"Austin, I'll holla man." Kilpatrick was moving toward his car.

"Ai'ight Dog."

"Oh, so you just gon' pretend like you don't know me Kilpatrick?" Jamie started crying.

He knew he had to react quickly before Austin caught on.

"Come on." He pulled her to the side.

"What did I do to you?" She continued to cry.

"You gon' have to chill with all that crying and shit. Where your peeps?" He looked over her toward her home. "What if they see you down here? You better go on back to the crib before you get in trouble Jamie. I'll call you."

"I thought you loved me! How could you just..."?

He snatched her by the arm throwing her against his car.

"Look girl! I got a woman with a baby on the way! And quit playin' on my muthafuckin' phone! You keep fuckin' with me..." he had to catch himself.

The only thing he could do at that point was leave. He jumped in his car, pulling off, leaving Jamie standing there holding her heart in her hands. His only intention was to shake her up enough to leave him alone. Never would he have thought he would be the one to witness the wickedness that resides in something so young.

Jamie stood there in astonishment, watching him speed away.

"We'll see if that woman has that baby Kilpatrick... Like I said before, you may not go with me...but I go with you!!" She turned and walked away wiping the tears from her eyes.

Austin peeked out the window watching Jamie walk away after observing the drama between her and his boy.

"Kilpatrick know damned well he done fucked that little girl, Ma." His mother was sitting in the living room area noddin', high off heroin.

"That nigga just don't know what he's done. Never fuck a spoiled, under-aged, brat!! Them type of chicks are crazy!" Austin concluded.

Extreme measures...

Jamie waited patiently for her parents to fall asleep, grabbed her mom's car keys and made her way out the door for the third night in a row. Jamie had been following Kilpatrick's girlfriend observing her nightly routine. Looking at the girl's size and age compared to Jamie's was one of the things that built her confidence; made her feel that she could easily abduct her. Jamie was convinced that as long as this girl was in the way she would always have problems with Kilpatrick. That was all Jamie needed to confirm and follow through with her plot.

Jamie continued to observe Kilpatrick's girlfriend's nightly routine. The girl would leave

Kilpatrick's mom's house around eleven to go to work. She worked midnights at a nursing home off Jefferson in Detroit. The girl was somewhere around 7 months pregnant and craved sweets before going into work. She would always stop at this donut shop a few blocks away from her job. This particular night, Jamie snuck off but wasn't able to go through with the plan. Just when Jamie was about to creep up on the girl in the parking lot, she surprised Jamie by walking out with one of her co-workers. Jamie was pissed; not knowing how many more times she would be able to sneak off with the car before her parents noticed.

Jamie had no choice other than to revert to *Plan A,* which meant, taking herself home and trying again tomorrow night. The only complicated task was trying to get home before her father woke up for his midnight snack.

It was around 12:45 a.m. and she was cutting it close. He usually gets up every night around 1:30 in the morning.

"Oh Shoot! It's almost 1:00! I can't believe this!" She said out loud in the car as she raced up the naked freeway that seemed deserted. Jamie didn't notice the State Trooper hiding in an underpass when she flew by. When he flashed his lights on her, she knew her driving days were over...

"Oh my God! What will I say! My parents are going to kill me!!!"

"License and registration young lady." The young handsome officer said kneeling down in her window.

Jamie could tell he was way too friendly by the way he was staring at her.

Maybe I could sweet talk him in to letting me go. "Officer?" she stared him in his eyes seductively. "I have a small problem."

"What could a beautiful tender..." he licked his lips..."Like you have a problem with?"

"I don't have license."

"You don't have license?"

"Please, just let me go Officer. My parents would kill me if they knew I had their car out this time of night."

"Wait, wait, wait a minute. Calm down. I'll tell you what. Why don't you take your keys out and follow me back to my car for a moment."

He moved away from her window, opening her door, gesturing his hand for her to go toward his police cruiser.

Jamie became nervous. She didn't know what his intentions were at that point. She wanted to believe it was all innocent; but from his behavior, it wasn't looking good.

Jamie got inside, overtaken by all the

electronic devices that surrounded the vehicle. She felt claustrophobic.

"Relax. I know your wondering why I asked you to come back to my vehicle. Let me relieve you by saying, I'm not taking you to jail. But, it's obvious that your parents don't know their car is missing. Am I right?"

Jamie put her head down looking like a child that had just been chastised.

"So, I guess to make this simple, you're going to need a favor from me. I don't usually do this kind of thing but I would be willing to bend the rules if you make it worth my while."

He started to unhook his holster, and then he unzipped his pants proceeding to pull out his flesh. Jamie was shocked seeing a man of his character take advantage of her this way! And the size of his penis was beyond what she had been used to. Jamie knew she had to calm down. If this was what she had to do to get out of her situation, he was on his way to heaven.

Jamie took hold of him in her hand and began to indulge; causing him to tremble as she imagined him as the one she loved. The officer was so into it, he didn't notice the other trooper pulling in behind him till after he filled Jamie's mouth with his salty residue.

"OH SHIT! HERE! Wipe your mouth with this!" The officer rushed to get himself together as the other officer was approaching.

"Frank?" The other officer called him pecking on his window.

"Hey Man! What's good?" He played it off rolling the window down.

"I was just checking on you, seeing if you needed some back up. What do you have there?" He looked over at Jamie who was sitting quietly trying not to give him eye contact.

"Ohhhh, just some teenager out here speeding with no license."

"Is that right?" The officer intercepted.

Jamie was shocked that he put her out there after he had just agreed to let her go. She was starting to feel betrayed.

"What do you think I should do with her?"

"Well, you can't let her drive herself away if she doesn't have license. How old is she?"

They both stared over at her waiting on a response. Jamie stared away looking out the window trying to strategize a way out of the situation.

"I think she's about 14 or 15. I'm going to look into it. But, I think I'm going to have to take her in."

"I'll follow you in. Just give me a signal when you're ready." The other officer tapped the inside door lining of the vehicle and walked away.

Jamie was fuming! She turned and stared at the officer who betrayed her, wanting to slice his penis off for leading her to believe she could trust him to let her go! He couldn't even look at her.

"I know you feel I misled you, but you can see I didn't have a choice in the matter."

He picked up the CB preparing to call in Jamie's parents' plates. Jamie pulled his arm forcing him to turn in her direction. To his surprise, she flashed him a mouth filled with his semen. He was astounded! His first reaction was to place the CB back against the attachment. He sat back in his seat and sneered then said, "Hold tight."

"Mmmhum." She folded her arms laying her back against the seat, twirling his semen around in her mouth.

Within seconds he came back to the vehicle, opened her door and instructed her to step out. Jamie followed his command. The officer was standing in front of her feeling uneasy. He didn't want his partner to notice his discomfort by him standing only a few feet away. The officer's first reaction was to take the professional approach with Jamie saying,

"You can go, but this is a warning. And don't let me catch you out here again or I won't hesitate to take you to jail the next time."

Jamie couldn't help but to stare at him contemplating on what she should do with her evidence. Judging by all the time that was lost she decided to walk away carelessly spitting the semen to the ground hoping the other officer noticed.

Jamie jumped in the car and sped off praying her dad had slept through his midnight snack.

A new day

Morning came and Jamie was relieved that her parents never noticed their car was missing. She was able to sneak in before her father made his way to the kitchen, which happened just as soon as she slid under her covers.

Jamie paced her bedroom floor all day until it was time to head out to handle some unfinished business.

As the night fell and her parents' snores turned into roars, Jamie assumed her position. Jamie sat in the parking lot of the donut shop in the dark looking around making sure no one was present when the girl came out. The only premise Jamie was working toward was having Kilpatrick all to herself.

As the girl exited the donut shop, never expecting anything evil was about to take place; she rubbed her stomach silently saying, "Mommy and Daddy can't wait for you to get here."

Those were her last words spoken to her unborn child. She would have never thought Kilpatrick would have placed her life in the hands of an enraged psychotic teenager.

As the girl placed the key in the door of her car, Jamie stepped out of the darkness hitting her so hard from behind, it knocked her out immediately.

"Slut! You're trying to take my man away from me!" Jamie retorted, taking a second glance around the parking lot before dragging the girl with all the strength she had to the back seat of her parent's car. She closed the back door and drove off to a dark, quiet place where she could be alone with her.

Jamie pulled in a park that had no lights working other than what reflected down from the full moon in the sky. She stared at the girl, flashing a light in her face, as she lay unconscious in the back seat. Jamie wondered what it was about her that her man liked.

"You're not even that pretty to me." Jamie said spitefully, stepping out the car, pulling the girl by her feet onto the wet, cold grass. Because the girl's head hit the edge of the car and the grass being so cold, she woke up hysterically, not remembering what happened to get her where she was.

"What the hell are you doing?" The girl struggled to speak. The flashlight Jamie had shining in her eyes obstructed her vision.

"Did you really believe I would allow you to have this baby and destroy what Kilpatrick and I have?"

That's when it hit the girl!

"Oh my God...you need some help. OOO!" She grunted in pain, holding her stomach. "My baby!" The girl yelled out trying to lift herself up from the wet grassy area.

Jamie showed no sensitivity toward the girl's situation. Something evil had invaded Jamie's spirit, and the only thing she wanted at that point was the girl's life.

The girl layed helplessly, balled up in a fetal position, locking her legs together trying to keep her baby from coming. Jamie stood over her watching her suffer. She knew no one would hear her out in the deep, dark, wooded park. Jamie had to make a decision as to how she was going to handle this before it had gotten too late.

Meanwhile, the girl tried to use what she had learned in Lamaze class to assist her with the contractions she was having. Jamie didn't know what to do! The last thing Jamie expected was labor happening right then!

The girl was wearing a maternity dress and was already in the position to have the baby. She became really scared. Her baby wasn't due for the next couple of months. She tried to hold back for as long as she could, but the pain wouldn't allow it. Within a few moments because of all the breathing and screaming, the baby had made its way out of the womb. Jamie grabbed a bag from the trunk of the car, rushing over to the girl trying to take the baby from her. The girl screamed in agony, holding on to her child as Jamie continued to pry the newborn from her hands! Jamie didn't notice at first that the baby was attached to a cord connected to the mother, which was one of the reasons the girl was screaming out in pain. The girl told her to cut the cord before her child dies! Jamie found something sharp, sliced the cord and then threw the newborn baby into the bag. The girl couldn't move and her screams were becoming weaker and weaker. She was losing a tremendous amount of blood. She kept begging Jamie to help her. Jamie lost focus! She left the girl at the park and drove off with the newborn baby in the back seat, being smothered in the plastic bag.

Jamie was in a state of shock. She didn't know what to do with the newborn that was no longer moving around in the bag. Somehow she ended up at a nearby hospital, taking the bag inside the emergency room, sitting it on the intake nurse's desk. Jamie couldn't hide the fact that she was covered in blood. The only thing she could do after realizing what she had done was fall to her knees in tears. All the nurses and doctors were called to the front when the intake nurse discovered what was inside the bag. They immediately went to work on the baby and did all they could do to revive it.

Jamie rocked back and forth, mumbling words they couldn't make out. From the looks of things, they thought she was the mother until she screamed out, "I HAD TO KILL THAT WOMAN!! SHE WAS GOING TO TAKE HIM AWAY FROM ME!!"

Within moments of trying to calm her down, they learned that the situation was much more than they anticipated.

Jamie later led the police to the girl's body, but time wasn't on her side. She had died an hour after Jamie left her there. The girl bled to death, perishing away on the cold grass.

Jamie's parents were informed of their daughter's arrest. It was basically nothing any one could do for her at that point. The authorities didn't hesitate taking her in. Jamie was charged with two murders. The baby died also.

Kilpatrick and his Mom were enraged. He had no idea that things were this out of control. He denied any allegations that stated he was involved with Jamie sexually. That was, of course, before Jamie tested positive on a pregnancy test during the physical she had to have when she was processed in the youth home.

He knew he couldn't deny Jamie any further. He had crossed enemy lines. Jamie's parents wanted to kill him, threatening to prosecute Kilpatrick for rape of a minor. His mom knew she couldn't afford to lose her son to the hands of society. She became active with Jamie's parents; doing all she could to support the situation, hoping they could one day forgive her son.

She then had to humble herself through Jamie's trial. Listening to the way Jamie tortured her son's girlfriend was extremely hard on her, but she had to face it. None of this helped the fact that Jamie was going to have a child by her son. Due to the circumstances that surrounded the situation; she realized that she had no choice other than to forgive and strive toward forgetting.

Jamie's crime was inhumane and brutal

according to the courts. They sentenced her to a juvenile detention center until she turned 21.

Once the baby was born, both Jamie's family and Kilpatrick's family shared custody of the child until Jamie finished her sentence.

Kilpatrick was still shook up about the whole situation. But he decided to take some responsibility and be a father to his child. He had a difficult time trying to build up enough strength to visit Jamie, but he felt that as he became closer to their beautiful daughter, En'Phinity Elese Jackson, the greater the possibility of him accepting Jamie as his baby's mama.

BE CAREFUL
WHAT U ASK 4 .

"There is no security between the cradle and the grave"

"EI"

"I ain't givin' that rat a dime!! On the real, that ugly muthafucka probably ain't mine anyway! I'm not buying no milk! I'm not buying no diapers! And I'm damned sure not bringing that thing home to my peeps! She set a brotha' up royally, Paul. I *hate* kids and them nasty bitches that be havin' um! I hope it die from crib death!" El was pacing the floor becoming more aggravated by the second.

"Man, first of all, calm yo' crazy ass down. You sound retarded, wishing death on an innocent child. That baby ain't ask to be here! What you need to do is take yo' ass over there and see that baby. I heard the little muthafucka look just like you. You might as well boss up fool. You knew that broad wasn't shit when you met her. Everybody in the hood don' hit that. The bitch got 9 kids by 9 different baby daddies! Any dude, I don't care how fine the bitch is, will throw a ski coat on before goin' up

1

in that pussy! You just got hood winked, baby! But, hold up, I gotta ask you this. Why would you hit it without a condom dawg? This is the same chick that I heard gave one of her kids away cause' it was ugly. And I know for a fact the other eight live with her Moms! She had to see you comin'. So face it, you got punk'd!" Paul said, laughing so hard he almost spilled his drink. "Better you than me, Chief."

"What time is it?" El asked finding no humor in what Paul had just said.

"I got 6:00." Paul held up his rose gold Rolex watch.

"Damn, it's still early."

"What you about to do, go kill 'em and throw their bodies in your trunk?" Paul teased.

"Fuck you! I'm out!"

El rushed up out of the bar before Paul could get another word in. Paul wasn't concerned about El doing anything to hurt the girl and her child so he ordered a few more drinks and took one of the chicks from the bar home afterwards.

El jumped into his 2005 Dodge Charger and flew up the Jeffries Freeway until he reached the Grand Boulevard exit. London stayed off of Rosa Parks and Hazelwood. El hadn't seen the baby since it was born so this would be their first encounter since she came home from the hospital.

London

Meanwhile, London was on the phone with her girl, Hunter, from around the way.

"Gurrrl... El is sick about this baby thang. I called him today and threatened to take him to court if he didn't bring some diapers and milk by here. You know the judge will be on my side."

"Whatever London. If anything they'll probably lock yo' crazy ass up and take yo' baby. Did you forget about your other nine kids?"

"What fuckin' nine kids! You know I don't claim my first. All my kids have good hair and look just like me. That first baby wasn't mine. I told you they switched my baby at the hospital. That's why I gave him away."

"Bitch, what the hell are you saying? You know what? You need a psychiatrist. And you better quit playin' with these cats out here. You gon' meet the wrong one. To keep it real, you might have met your match, 'cause that fool you don' had that baby by is insane." Hunter felt uncomfortable with her statement.

Hunter knew how El was cut, and this could be seriously dangerous for her friend. In spite of the fact that her girl was missing a few screws; Hunter knew El had no conscience or patience when it came to dealing with London.

London ignored the baby crying in her crib and continued her conversation saying, "The only thing that I'm worried about is dude quitting his job. This is all about the paper chase Ma. Do you think I wanted another mouth to feed? Hell Naww! As greedy as my ass is! You know I ain't got no time to be playing Mama up in this bitch. This is business and this cat gon' pay me swell before it's over."

"Do you have any feelings for him London?"

"I think I do. You know I like a lot of attention and I think he will be the one to give it to me. I really feel he's the one that will take me out of these crack infested apartments and place me up in some glamour shit."

"THE PLANE! THE PLANE!" Hunter yelled, laughing. "I know you remember that little midget on Fantasy Island right?"

"So what are you saying Hunter?"

"Bitch, yo' plane just landed and that little muthafucka is the pilot. Call me when you come back from vacation." (CLICK)

El drove into the parking lot of London's apartment building. He stared up on her balcony to see if it looked like she was home; then called her from his cell phone.

"Hello?" London reluctantly answered.

"Open the door." He hung up making his way inside her building.

"My dick is here! My dick is here!" She ignorantly crooned as she made her way toward the crying child to calm her. "Shhhh, hush Camay your daddy's here." She picked her up and pulled her close. The baby had been crying for so long she was trembling in her arms.

El wasn't coming for no conversation; strictly demands. But as soon as London opened the door and he saw the baby clutched in her arms, the feeling of anger slowly started to fade.

"You came to see your baby?" London moved aside to let him in.

"I ain't come here to see shit. You…"

"Shhhhh. You gon' make her start whining again. I just got her to shut up." London demanded pulling the blanket away from the baby's caramel skin. The only thing you could see outside of the baby's fat cheeks was her beautiful black rich hair that was just like his. He stood in the doorway staring like he had just laid eyes on a suitcase filled with cash. She was the most gorgeous creature he could have ever laid eyes on. All the bitterness he had inside was overwhelmed by a stubborn kind of love that was fighting to make its way to the surface.

"Why are you staring at her like that? She yours! Here!" London shoved the baby into his arms. He tried to move away, but London basically forced the baby on him; almost dropping her in the process. Luckily he didn't resist.

"I didn't come here to make no claim. I'm here to get some shit straight." He said staring between London and the baby.

"You could start by having a seat and feeding that baby. Shit, I'm tired! I've been up all night with your brat. You came just in time to help. Maybe I can do some things for myself now." London walked away on purpose. She had already prepared herself for this visit.

El was experiencing something unexpected. There was some type of connection between him and the child that he couldn't comprehend at that moment. He slowly walked over and carefully sat down staring into her eyes. He was wondering how he could have been so bitter and angry toward something so innocent and beautiful. It was at that point that he knew the time had come for him to face his responsibility. Though it would take time and tolerance to have to deal with the mother of his child; Camay was his first and he thought that time would hopefully heal all wounds.

London knew the longer Camay stayed attached to El's arms the more difficult it would be for him deny her.

El sat there staring at the baby watching her squirm and make all kinds of sounds. London was in the kitchen preparing a bottle of milk. Still lost in admiration, El took the baby's fingers and placed his index finger between them. He snuck a smile in as he watched her innocently.

When London walked in the living room and saw how El was enjoying his one-on-one with his child, it set off a jealousy that could not be described.

I didn't have your ass for him to fall in love with you! This is about me and him. You better watch yourself you little witch! London hatefully and silently thought about her own flesh and blood. She knew if she didn't check herself, the worst was yet to come. So she faked like she usually does when things happen that challenge her sanity.

"So…now you wanna' play Daddy." She rudely passed him the bottle.

"Just show me how to do this." He snatched the bottle out of her hand.

"Boy please! What could be so difficult

about sticking a damned bottle in a baby's mouth?"

El ignored her sliding the nipple of the bottle into the baby's mouth. He thought it was strange how things were unfolding. At first, he was planning on going over there to pounce on London's head not knowing at the time that he would find peace right in his arms.

London was trying to get a word in or two and he tuned her out while feeding Camay. That set off a rage in her that caught his attention.

"You act like you didn't want shit to do with *us*. Now you over here playing, Daddy Day Care."

El's two-way-pager went off. He stood with the baby in one arm as he checked his message. Still ignoring London, he walked into the bedroom where she had a basinet set up for Camay, gently laid her inside and watched her sleep for a couple of seconds.

Don't worry little Momma. I'll be back to get you.

Those were his last words before he made his way to the door.

"Oh! So you just gon' leave! How the fuck are you!"

"Shut the hell up before you wake the..." He caught himself. "You know what. I don't owe you no explanation. I'm out." He went to turn the doorknob.

"Fuck you! You trick ass bum! You just gon' come in here and hold that baby and not say one word to me! What the fuck am I? A one-night-stand?"

"You sick London."

That just caused the volcano to erupt. She flipped, causing a scene with the neighbors and people that were coming in and out of the building. He made his way down the steps shaking his head in disgust.

What have I gotten my dick into?

El was moving as fast as he could toward his car. London ran out on her balcony that sat on the fourth floor of her apartment yelling and cursing. She had become a mad woman and that troubled him.

"Take yo' dumb ass back in there! You're making a fool out of yourself."

"Fuck You! You ain't shit, El!"

"You know what London. The next time I see Camay will be in court. You're not fit for no kids! You fucked up in the head!" El went to turn his back for a hot minute. Within a few seconds, before he was able to place his key in the car door, London did something to him that changed his life forever…

"OH! YOU WANT CUSTODY OF THIS

THANG! HERE! CUSTODY GRANTED MUTHAFUCKA!!!"

Everything from that point was like slow motion. London slung the innocent soul over the balcony tossing the baby from four stories high to death. El did all he could to save the child. He couldn't get to her in time to catch her. Now her small body lay lifeless on the sidewalk of a fallen dream.

Be careful what you ask for…

AN OPEN DOOR

*"**Anger** is one letter short of **Danger**"*

Choyce

"You have a collect call from Reg… an inmate at the Delport Correctional Facility. To accept this call please press zero. If you do not wish to…." I nervously pressed zero.

"Hello?" I answered with an uneasy tone.

"Choyce! Wha'dup!" The deep threatening voice responded on the other end.

"I don't know. You tell me!"

"You left word for me to holla at you. Talk to me Ma."

"Let me get straight to the point. I heard that you were upset with me. Sole' approached me the other day saying something about you heard I was out here spittin' venom in the streets about you. I don't even know you to be…"

"Whoa, whoa, hold up Ma." He cut me off. "This is my first time hearing this. You said Sole' told you what? And when?"

"Yesterday, when I was on the block, I was like, spittin' venom? She agreed, and I told her to give you my number so we can

1

straighten this out."

"She lied to you baby girl. Wrong Nigga."

Do you know I believed dude? I didn't see any reason for him to lie about something like this. I mean, what fool would say anything about this crazy nut? Everybody in the hood was scared of Reg. His real name was Regnad but I heard he hated to be called that so everyone called him Reg.

Dude had all kinds of rumors out on the streets about how he used to torture some girl he was messin' with before he went to prison. He was mad crazy over this chick. I didn't know her personally, but word was out how jealous he was over her. Rumor had it that he crushed her fingers with a hammer for not returning his phone call one night. The last I heard, girlfriend was in hiding.

Regnad's name spoke volumes in the hood. And like a woman that fell in love with the devil, I became enslaved forever. I had no reason to believe this was all a setup. And from that point, I received an open invitation to death before my 21st birthday.

*****

Reflecting back in time…I can remember just like it was yesterday…how I wanted to be had by any and every guy that was selling drugs or called himself a thug. *A 'hood rat'* was a better way to define my personality, 'cause I was so damned stupid! All the locals would swing by my crib in the middle of the night just to get some head. I have to admit, I was the bomb; learned from the best. But, the sad part of it all was, I wasn't makin' no money!

Regnad and I never kicked it during the late 90s. He had this thing for light skinned women. If it was all about a freak that gave some bomb ass head, I would've had him a long time ago. But none of that fazed him. It was something about them red-boned women that catered to his every need. A chocolate sister like myself, couldn't do nothin' for him.

Anyway, I didn't sweat it, but I couldn't resist the fantasies I was having of one day having him all to myself. I just didn't think the day would fall under life threatening circumstances.

Meanwhile, the collect calls had started to build up and Regnad and I had become closer. He set up a bogus phone line to keep me from having to stand on the corner of the Lodge and 7 Mile with an "I'll Work for Food" sign 'cause my parents would have freaked out and put me out if they had seen collect calls from a prison on their phone bill!

The conversations we had convinced me

3

that he was nothing like he used to be five years ago. I fell in love with what *I* thought he had become.

After all the nice letters and pictures he had sent to me, the day I had been anticipating on had finally arrived...

"MY VISITOR'S PASS!"

Visiting Regnad was something I had desperately been waiting for!

He had enclosed some instructions, purposely smothered in his cologne that read:

Choyce, when you come down, don't wear no panties. And make sure whatever you put on has easy access. I'll take it from there...Reg.

His wish was my command. I didn't waste any time finding the right outfit to wear just for the occasion. I couldn't wait 'til Friday rolled around.

*****

Regnad had just been placed in a camp after serving time in a maximum-security facility. He told me all kinds of unbelievable stories like the one about lifers and people on death role. He said that if America goes into a do or die war, officers will receive a direct order to kill them because they are considered the enemy. I didn't believe it until I went and looked it up at the library. *I wonder who created that law?*

*****

Regnad explained in his letters how this camp was setup. As I was making my way down the road to see him, I had a picture stored in my mind from the description he gave in his letters.

Once I made it to the gate that surrounded the camp, it was everything he described. A guard had to drive me along with other visitors up to the entrance. On my way up to see him, I became nervous and insecure about my love handles and flat behind. But, once I made it there, none of that mattered. He treated me like a queen. He held me, kissed me and caressed me discreetly. He informed me before his hands caressed my body that if the Correctional Officer were to catch us, they would terminate our visit. I didn't want that.

After all the touching and teasing, the sneaking and the freaking made things more interesting. I was hooked after what he had done to me. I felt loved and appreciated for once in my life. His past was no longer an issue with me. In my eyes he was a new man and no one, at that point, could have told me differently.

*****

"Spread that pussy for me." He demanded with aggression.

Regnad took control and I loved it. I just happened to be one of those girls that loved me a roughneck. I'm talking about the ones that would throw you against the wall, strip off your clothes or smack you on your ass during sex! This kind of thing did something to my sexual drive.

I did everything he told me to do as we sat a picnic table out of sight.

"Make sure you keep those eyes on them C.O.s."

In a way I felt a little uncomfortable, but after his tongue slid inside of me, I lost sight of my surroundings. He had me hemmed up on a picnic table between trees doing his thang. My legs were gapped open with my thighs and legs dangling over his shoulders. The boy was a magician! I was mesmerized by the way his muscular arms were gripped tightly around my hips. I found myself rotating my hips, following the flow he had going on with his tongue. It was like harmony.

Well, the show was over and I admit we were very lucky none of the correctional officers caught us. I had the pleasure of coming twice and enjoying the rest of the visit.

When it was time for me to leave I really didn't want to go. I had become attached in one visit! I felt like Regnad had changed my life. It was just too soon to tell what those changes were...

*****

That day finally rolled around for me, and my baby to put it down in the real world! Regnad was only hours away from freedom and knocking my walls in! Our relationship had grown secretly. I never shared what we had with no one. He insisted on that. He bluntly said that I ran my mouth too much. He felt women are made to listen, and speak when spoken to. He had a point. I did talk too much and most of the time I didn't know what the hell I was talking about! Either way, I thought he was worth it, so I stopped gossiping and telling my business to strangers.

*****

My phone rang and I anxiously answered; surprised that it was his brother calling me.

"Choyce, Reg is coming home and he needs us to pick him up."

"What? I thought...never mind. What time?" I asked, confused. I thought he had his own way home. This was all together new to me, but I desperately wanted to see him, so I ignored any strange feelings I had about it and followed Regnad's request.

His brother continued, "We need to be there around nine, he said."

"9 o'clock in the morning?"

"No baby, at night."

"Be where?"

"He said he will meet us at a liquor store off 24 north, not too far from the prison."

"Okay. I'll pick you up at seven. It takes at least an hour and a half to get there."

"Bet."

Thinking nothing strange about the arrangements, I picked Drake up and we made our way down the highway. Once we pulled into the place where Regnad told us to be, we ended up waiting a couple of hours for him, but he never showed up. I questioned Drake over and over, making sure we were at the right location. We were both sitting there like two niggers in a country town. I was becoming very uncomfortable.

"Drive up this road to see if we see him." Drake directed.

"All right."

As we went back and forth up the dark road that surrounded the prison camp, I never once thought something was a little peculiar about the whole situation.

"Who the hell is that?"

Drake and I saw a white man with a black baseball cap and coat rise up out of some bushes, then disappeared back into them. We had come to realize that Regnad was nowhere to be found and jumped back on the highway.

*****

Days had gone by and still no word from Regnad. I was beginning to think something had happened to him till my pager went off showing a number I wasn't familiar with.

"Hampton Inn." A white lady greeted.

I was confused at first not noticing the three-digit code behind the number. I asked the clerk to transfer me to what appeared to be a room number.

"Yeah." A deep familiar voice answered.

"I know this is not you, Nigga!"

"Come see me."

"I'm gon' come see you alright!"

I can't believe Regnad! Of all the nerve he had to do me this way! I needed to calm down. It wasn't like I was upset, more worried than anything.

He gave me directions to the hotel and I was there in less than thirty minutes. When I knocked at his room door, he opened it surprising me standing there naked, exposing every muscular part of his body. I started to tingle all over, saying to myself,

He did that!

"Hey you." He smiled.

I had to play it off, like I wasn't fazed by his naked approach. That's some shit I would do! "Don't hey you me! I can't believe you!"

I walked past him throwing my hand up like the drama queen I was. As I turned around to face him, he was all over me kissing my lips, pressing his teeth into my neck, and then biting my nipples through my blouse.

"You *sss mmm*...you think you *mmm*..."

I couldn't utter another word. He lifted me in his arms, and laid me on the bed. He made love to me. I was a little disappointed that he didn't knock the bottom out! He had just gotten out of prison! Five years with no pussy?

He became a little aggressive with my kitten when I threw my hips into him, letting him know to handle my shit like a real one! That's when he threw me in all kids of positions.

That's was more like it...

This was the only night I could remember us being together as one...

I ended up staying at the hotel with him for a few nights. Then he had some business to attend to with a couple of his boys and promised me we'd hook up in a few days. I respected that, being that he was down for so long. I told him to do his thang and I made my way back home. My only concern was the lack of respect his friends had for me. There was no doubt in my mind that Dino and Larry wasn't going to snitch me out. We had a threesome way before Regnad's time and I prayed that wouldn't change the way he looked at me.

*****

"Reg! I can't believe you're fucking that ho' man! Everybody had a piece of that pussy." Dino said, sitting in the back of Larry's truck, counting his stash.

Larry, on the other hand, was driving with them in the car to Bloomfield Hills to pick his daughter up from private school.

"I'm gon' say this one time Chief." Regnad retorted, turning his head toward the back seat to face Dino. "I don't give a fuck what she did before me. Don't bring me shit unless I inquire about it." Regnad's tone was threatening.

Dino paused for a second, swallowing his pride and went back to counting his cash.

"Now," Regnad turned his attention back to Larry that was laughing at what he said to Dino. "What chu' need me to do El?" Regnad questioned.

"This eastside nigga trying to move in on my territory. You know how I am about my money!" Regnad nodded in agreement. "I got everything you left me with and then some to complete the job. After I pick up my baby-girl, we'll shoot by there and tighten you up, Friend." Larry said with confidence.

"You know I likes' my shit to be organized. Let me know all that's needed to be done so I can get this over with. How much paper you talking."

"Fifty G's."

"How you want 'um? Dead, cripple, or a vegetable? Holla at me!"

"For fifty grand, I want to 'tend that nigga's funeral and fuck his wife afterwards."

"Then let's get down to business."

*****

Four days went by and I hadn't seen nor heard from Regnad. The last thing I would of thought was he was chilling with one of his old flames. I trusted him when he said he was only taking care of business.

Saturday night had rolled around and one of my girls traded vehicles with me. She had a black truck that went well with this outfit I had on. So while she went to work in my ride, I had planned to hang out in hers. I called up my girl, Kia, to go out with me to this party in Southfield. I never made it. Before I could pull out of the driveway, Regnad had blocked me in.

"Choyce! Where you going?" He yelled out the passenger window of Larry's BMW.

"Out... You've been ghost for a couple of days."

I rolled my eyes as he approached me. It was late and I was dressed to kill. He stared me up and down; throwing on that sexy smile that damned near had me on my knees. My plans were already cancelled before he asked...

"You coming with me?"

"Nope. I'm going with Casper."

"Who the fuck is Casper?"

"The friendly damned Ghost." I responded sarcastically.

He didn't find any humor in my Casper comment. I could tell Regnad wasn't used to being rejected. He never accepted it by any one with out consequences.

"Oh, you got jokes?"

"No. I have an attitude. Where you been?"

"We'll talk in yo' ride."

He grabbed a shovel and a duffle bag from his boy's car and threw it in the back of the truck. I was oblivious to what his need for that stuff was!

Who did he think he was to invite himself in a truck that wasn't even mine?

Regnad had this disgusted look on his face when he got inside. I didn't know what to make of it, so I just brushed it off. He told Larry he was out and the rest was a question of sanity.

"Whose ride is this?"

"A friend."

"You know what I used to do to women that talked to me like that?"

"Enlighten me."

"Let's go." He ignored me.

After staring at him a few seconds, I forgot about the shit in the back and him being MIA for the last four days. I was willing and ready to be with my Boo. That distance between us did something to me. I missed him and was just happy to be in his presence. So I decided to leave my attitude in the driveway before we pulled off.

As I started backing out, I thought about my friend Kia. I was supposed to pick her up.

Oh well KiKi. My man comes first Boo Boo.

Driving up my street preparing to start our journey to 'I don't know where', he started acting strange. That's when I realized he wasn't the same man I went to see in prison.

"What's going on Reg? What's that for?" I questioned nervously after he pulled a machine gun from his duffle bag.

"Don't ask questions. Just drive."

All of a sudden Regnad became this different person and he was scaring the hell out of me! He barely said a word other than giving directions to where he wanted me to go. I couldn't help but stare at him in disbelief! The large metal machine gun that was resting on his lap told me this would have been one night I would never forget. My whole life flashed before me! Nothing he had said from that point made sense.

"I guess you're wondering what the fuck I'm doing, huh?"

He never once looked at me. I was afraid to follow any further instructions that may have led me deeper into his vindictive scheme. Hell, there I was, driving a truck that wasn't mine, loaded with God knows what, and he's asking me what I'm wondering! I just nodded yes, and continued to follow his directions.

"You know, Choyce. I don't know how to tell you this, but... I am a very evil and vengeful person. I think I got that from my mother. She used to beat the hell out of me when I was young. FOR NOTHING!" He hit the dashboard startling me. "FOR FUCKIN' NOTHIN'! Then when my Uncle would come up to visit and ask to take us hunting with him. You know that bitch wouldn't let me and my brothers go. So instead of allowing me to hunt animals, she'd rather see me hunt human beings. I'm a predator. And when you cross me...you die..."

I didn't want him to smell my fear. I had to speak my mind and deal with the consequences later. I just prayed I would live behind them.

"I can see you've been through a lot, Reg. But, sometimes we have to forgive and move on. Humble ourselves; let go baby. You just got out of prison, come on now! Why would you subject yourself to more malice that could place you right back in the same position you were in before? Think about it. Don't do anything that could jeopardize your freedom. I care about you, Reg. And I really wanted to see us make it. But right now, you're scaring me." I took a deep breath, hoping I got through to him.

He hadn't heard a word I said. Talking to him was useless. His mind was made up.

"Do you want to know the truth about why I was doing time?"

I shook my head, no.

"I was in love with this dumb ass broad that set me up royally! Bitch! I swear if I see her, I'm gon' kill her! I would have given her the world until that shit went down in Atlanta. We had a run we were doing together. It was worth 280 G's! She had this wealthy ass uncle that kept a safe filled with cash! The plot was for us to go down there and rob and kill him! Instead, I take my black ass down there and end up being at the wrong place at the wrong muthafuckin' time. Come to find out, the bitch set me and her uncle up. The FEDS raided the house the same day I ran up in there with the heat about to handle my business. I got 9 years for that ho' ass shit! And you know what that bitch got? Immunity... case closed..."

My ears were starting to hurt listening to him. I thought dude had changed. All of his letters, his conversations, and the weekend visits to see him didn't mean a damned thang! I thought it was real. He seemed so sincere.

"Reg, I don't want no part of this. It sounds like a personal issue between you and your lost love. I want a life and I love my freedom. If you want to track down some bitch that'll cost you your freedom, that's on you. I'll still write you and you can still call me collect. But I'm not trying to become no jail trustee for the rest of my life." I tried to get my point

17

across under pressure.

My heart was racing extremely fast!

I slowed down, pulling to the side of the curve. I thought I had made a point.

"It's too late to make sense of this Choyce. I got to do what I got to do. So, either you make this right down this street, or you die with the bitch."

My feet became numb and my head started spinning. The only thing I could think of was living at that very moment. The way he was comfortably holding his gun pointed in my direction, I didn't even second-guess making that turn.

Regnad had me pull up on the side of an alley and park. He got out and disappeared into the darkness carrying his gun. I wanted to pull off and leave, but I was scared for my life and the lives of my family! He would have easily found me and wouldn't have hesitated taking me out! My body was cold. I was beyond paranoid. Then I heard shots! I cried, locking the doors! I felt like I was foolishly waiting to die!

As Regnad reappeared, he wasn't alone. There was someone with him. A woman.

"Open the muthafuckin' door!" He snapped, hitting the steel against the window, restraining this distraught woman with his free hand.

I unlocked the door.

"GET CHO' ASS IN THERE!" He threw her inside. She was crying just as hard as I was.

"WHAT THE FUCK ARE YOU CRYING FOR! THIS AINT ABOUT YOU!" He looked at me crazy.

"I-I-I'm sorry…." I stuttered, placing the truck in drive not knowing where the hell I was going, so I asked.

"Just drive the muthafucka anywhere!"

The girl was balled up in the back, trembling profusely. I could make out in the rear view mirror that she was a light complexion young woman, overtaken by fear.

"YOU DIDN'T HAVE TO KILL HIM REGNAD! HE WAS INNOCENT!!" She cried hysterically.

I couldn't believe she called him by his whole name. This had to have been the woman he had mentioned betrayed him.

What other fool would be that suicidal to call him Regnad?

I didn't know what to do at that point. I tried to stay off busy streets to avoid police. I felt they would arrest me as an accessory. I was confused and I didn't know which way to turn. Then, out of nowhere, he snapped!

"BITCH! SHUT THE FUCK UP!" He laid his gun down and tore the paneling trying to get to her! I felt helpless. "You caused this shit HO'!" SMACK!!

He was beating the hell out of her! I yelled for him to stop, but he ignored me! She was screaming and crying so loud I could feel each blow he inflicted on her! She was trying to fight him back, but he was too strong for her and it only made things worst.

"I'M GON' TEACH YOU A LESSON! YOU GON' SUFFER JUST LIKE I DID! YOU-- SMACK!! THOUGHT--SMACK!! I--SMACK!! WOULD LET--SMACK!! YOU GET AWAY-- SMACK!! WITH THAT SHIT, HUH!!!!--SMACK!! I BROKE OUT OF JAIL TO GET TO YO' ASS!!!"

Did he just say, broke out of jail???

A part of me couldn't help but to concentrate on his fist falling into her face repeatedly, but the "breaking out of jail" part? Oh, hell no! I was about to lose my mind. It was too much and I had to do something.

Regnad's arm moved up and down through the rearview mirror, causing me to damned near hit a parked car! Then I heard something ripping! He had torn her shirt from her body along with her skirt that finely draped her wide hips.

Is this nigga about to rape her?
I asked myself as I was continuing to swerve almost losing control. I could tell he was holding her mouth to silence her screams. That's when I verified what he was doing. He pulled his pants down throwing her legs over his shoulders. I could see her scratching and hitting his chest trying to fight him off as he tore his way inside of her. I felt sick. I couldn't believe he used me to get to her this way. It was like I wasn't there. She was still crying and it was obvious he was violating her. Somewhere in between, she couldn't fight anymore and at one point I thought he had killed her! I could no longer drive. The truck was parked and I had completely turned around in my seat to look at him. He was like an animal tearing into someone's flesh. He was biting and sucking her nipples like he was trying to tear them away from her skin! In spite of her not reacting to his repulsive act, he kept his speed. Her head was hitting the paneling from him pushing his way in to her aggressively. He was a madman and I just couldn't stomach it anymore! I grabbed the gun he left unsecured and raised it at him.

"Get the fuck off of her Regnad." He ignored me, grunting, releasing all the pain he selfishly believed she caused. I repeated myself, "I'm going to say this one more time." I cocked the gun. That's when he knew it wasn't a game. "Get... the fuck... up NOW!" He eased himself out of her, and then shoved her onto the floor like a piece of trash.

I saw something in his eyes that read,

"Bitch! You better pull that trigger 'cause if you don't, you gon' die...."

What he failed to realize was, I was dead when he stepped foot in this truck. There was no doubt in my mind he wasn't going to kill me after witnessing that.

Then out of nowhere!

"PAP! PAP! PAP!" Blood splattered across the back window. I dropped the gun to the floor and fell into the driver's seat covering my mouth, eyes wide.

"You okay Alysha?" A woman's voice yanked the door open, pulling Regnad's limp body out the truck after placing two bullets in his chest, then one in his head. She pulled the girl from off the floor, taking hold of her, and her clothing.

"You Muthafucka!" The woman spit on him. "I can't believe he did this to you, Alysha!" The woman cried.

I sat in awe. I didn't realize that my life was so close to being taken until this woman appeared like a hero in an action packed movie! I had frozen up, scared to pull the trigger. Regnad knew this. There was no doubt in his mind I would have choked up. He was for sure to have had two dead females on his hands.

Now I know what the shovel was for.

*****

The woman who saved our lives was a close acquaintance of Regnad's ex, Alysha. I learned a whole new story after that night. I was thankful that Alysha was vigilant enough to explain to the girl that I was a victim like she was.

Anyway, the story...

Regnad had caught a case for something totally different than what he had told me. He killed two guys on the eastside for staring at Alysha's behind. He was able to get the case reduced to manslaughter and was sentenced to 9 to 15 years in a state prison. He couldn't live with the fact that Alysha would be out in the streets where he couldn't keep his jealous eyes on her. He was extremely insecure about her being with someone else. So he lied, saying she was an accessory to his crime, forcing her to have to do 24 months in jail. She was upset that he played her like that, but she felt trapped. He physically abused her so much that she was scared to plead her innocence in spite of the circumstances.

Regnad had to pull 9 years before he was eligible for parole. When he went up for his parole hearing, they gave him an additional two-year hit because of his habitual misbehavior and some majors he received while he was incarcerated.

Regnad was furious with the decision of the parole board! He was anticipating coming home even more since Alysha had officially broken it off with him before she was released. It wasn't the fact that she left him that he felt warranted his immediate attention. It was why and whom she left him for.

Alysha was all about Regnad during her first 10 months of her sentence. She had read his letters of apology, promises and commitments. She was willing to try again with him till she met Jenette, also in custody.

Jenette wasn't your average lesbian. She had class about herself. The image she portrayed defined her personality as above average. She carried a reputation that never lacked respect and to many, including Alysha, she was very attractive.

Alysha never saw herself with a woman, and from time to time, she found herself wondering what it was about Jenette that made her fall in love. But, Alysha knew this was one secret she wouldn't be able to hide for long. So she wrote Regnad and told him. She didn't want to lie to him anymore. He had been wondering why her letters went from full pages, to one or two lines, then to none. And once he received conformation on her end, his life changed for the worst! He felt betrayed, angered, and vengeful. That's when he made a decision to break out of jail, injuring three officers in the process. Regnad was determined to get back what he thought he owned. Once he had got out on the streets and learned of Alysha's whereabouts, I was his open door.

The night of the nightmare, Regnad ended up shooting Alysha's brother twice leaving him for dead. Thank God the brother survived long enough to follow Regnad and Alysha, seeing the truck he had taken her hostage in.

Jenette came in and noticed a blood trail that led her to Alysha's half-conscious brother who was lying in the alley fighting for his life. He was able to give Jenette enough information that led her to the truck we were being victimized in. Jenette didn't hesitate killing the man that her girl has been hiding from since the day they met.

MONTHS LATER....

I sat back in my car alone staring at the lake.

I'm lucky to be alive!

I haven't been able to sleep well since the incident with Regnad. What he did was immoral and evil and it still haunts me to this very day. The deeper my thoughts, the more his face appeared in my mind. I tried to focus my attention on something else, like them damned seagulls that were flying over my head! But, as I stared through my rearview mirror, I noticed something about this sign that stood out. It read:

DANGER! NO SWIMMING IN LAKE!

It was the word *danger* that grabbed my attention. It gave me this feeling of something wicked. I felt I was being watched through the eyes of the 6-letter word. It was like it was trying to warn me of someone's presence. Then it hit me!

REGNAD...DANGER...spelled backwards! Oh my God! The signs were always there! How could I have not seen them? How could I have been so blind?

A Church Vixen

"And God gave them over the shameful lust. Even their women exchanged natural relations for unnatural ones. In the same way the men also abandoned natural relations with women and were inflamed with lust for one another."

Romans 1:26-27

*****

"Let the church say AMEN!"

"AMEN!!" The congregation screamed loudly.

"I said...let the church say AMEN!"

"AMEN!" They all stood to their feet glorifying and ready to worship and praise the man that stood before the cross.

Just like a drama-filled movie or a good book, it has to start off with a BANG to grab your attention. This is one of the many mind-fabricated techniques that are used in the house of the Lord.

There are five oppressing aspects about a church filled with over five hundred to a thousand members...Hypocrisy...Control... Manipulation...Capital...and Men on The Down Low...

I've been a member of several churches and I can confirm that the devil walks in

1

countless shoes. Many of my personal church acquaintances say Hell carries my size. I just simply tell them, if the shoe doesn't fit, they must acquit!

I can't help the fact that I'm a gay man that has a fetish for spiritual men! I've been trying to give it to God since my first sexual encounter with a pastor of one of the neighborhood's *popular* churches, but it seemed like the more I tried, the easier I found myself being taken by another man of God. I know it's the challenge that makes it so interesting. It doesn't take much to impress me. He could quote a few scriptures from the Bible and get my money, my trust and everything I own by the end of service.

The most complicated part about being involved with this type of men was falling in love. When we're together I feel safe and secure. Whatever I'm struggling with doesn't matter because they make it seem like nothing's wrong. They tell me God will forgive us and from that point, I become the next best thing to their wives.

I've had many sexual experiences with pastors, deacons and other flings under these million dollar safe havens. Every time a new church is built, I'm trying to become a member.

Back in the day they used to call me a

gay-ho'-hopper. Now I'm what I call a down-low-church-anal-popper! I know what I'm saying may sound evil to many and somewhat unrealistic. But I'll tell you this without going into further detail; I've been to many of your homes. I've sat and ate at many of your tables. And most of all, I've slept with several of them big time preachers I'm sure most of you have had your damned self.

I don't know about you, but I will never reveal my identity. I would rather die in peace than to be sitting on the *Top 10 National Best Seller List* next to the chick that wrote *The Video Vixen*. I'd die for sure if I were to expose the men I've slept with in the churches right here in *your* city! So let me leave you with this...

Never place your trust in man, for he may betray you. And don't forget, the Devil carries shoes in women's sizes too...

Taken Over

"Be careful who you leave to care for your child…."

******

"Here girl!"

Nicolas tossed Terra enough crack to hold her over for a couple of hours. There was only one thing on her mind…smoking till the sun came up.

It's amazing how drugs can make a person forget about all things that are important; like Terra's 10-year-old daughter, Kemora, who was now being taken advantage of by a man that claimed he would never betray a friend's trust.

*****

"Come on! Come on!" Terra became irritated with the lighter. There wasn't enough fuel in it to tilt in a corner. She shook it, turned it upside down, and then threw it against the wall, hoping it would give flame long enough to provide her body with a high that was more advanced than the one she had the night before.

Nicolas left Terra enough drugs to keep her busy while he crept up the steps to Kemora's room.

Kemora lay in her bed shaking like a leaf on a tree. She knew it was around the time for the twenty-four year old man to make his way into her space. This abuse had been going on over six months since her father, Jay, went away to prison.

Jay trusted Nicolas with his life. He just knew he could depend on him to be there for his family. There were never any signs of treachery on Nicolas' part and that was all Jay felt he needed to look for in a friend.

Nicolas, on the other hand had always had this sick desire to be with Jay's daughter; as early as six years of age. He felt the child was in love with him and wanted him just as badly as he wanted her. Now with Terra on drugs, Nicolas had them both under his control.

As soon as Kemora's door slowly pushed open, tears formed in her eyes. She wanted to scream, but she knew it could have been dangerous. So she muffled her cries and began to pray.

Nicolas pulled the edge of Kemora's cover up, climbed under them and did his thang.

Prayers unanswered.

*****

How they met....

Nicolas had been around long before Jay married Terra or Kemora was even thought of. They both grew up together off of Holcomb and Mack. Nicolas always seemed to be a responsible, well kept, individual that had never crossed him in the past. So Jay had no problem bringing him around after he had gotten married.

When Kemora was born and had sprouted up like a little lady, she was hardly around, finding comfort in staying with her grandmother most of the time. Jay had no way of knowing his friend had a sick kind of love for his child.

A few years after Jay and Nicolas had built this brotherly bond; Jay got caught with a large amount of cocaine, forcing him into a plea agreement that stripped away 58 years of his freedom. Terra gave up hope on life and instead of turning to God; she found heaven in her addiction to drugs. Sadly, Nicolas was the one to blame for her careless decision. He observed how weak and vulnerable Terra had become and used that as the perfect opportunity to persuade her to use drugs.

Terra was considered Jay's backbone before any of this had taken place. He fell in

3

love with something that was far past beauty.
She was considered an asset to him.

Terra carried a credit score as high as an
850. Jay always felt there was nothing more to
life than a woman with good credit and stability.
To him that defined honesty and self-respect.

Having to leave his family was difficult for
Jay, but he felt a part of him would still be there
if Nicolas had taken over.

Nicolas gave his word he wouldn't let him
down. He promised to provide for his family
while he was away. Now everything in life that
once meant something to Jay, Terra and
Kemora was up to the devil.

*****

"NICOLAS!" Terra yelled out loud. She
was frustrated with that darn lighter! Terra was
in the basement recreation area, yelling up the
steps.

Nicolas thought he heard something and
reacted quickly. He couldn't risk being caught in
Kemora's bedroom so he pulled Kemora's
gown back over her, tossing a blanket on top of
her small frame whispering, "Shh, you stay put.
Not one word…or else."

Kemora then turned over on her side
staring out the window into the stars confused,
wondering why life has to be so complicated.

Nicolas decided not to chance going back up to Kemora's room after being interrupted by Terra. She was so upset about having to fight to get high that he felt it was best to hang around her.

Nicolas gave Terra another lighter, watching her anxiously light her pipe. She invited the smoke filled contents into her soul, coughing from the greed of wanting it all at one time. He smirked, and then nodded his head, walking over to the pool table to shoot a few rounds. Terra was smoking so fast he made an attempt to stop her by saying,

"Yo baby, you better chill before you overdose." He glanced over at her noticing her smoking two rocks at a time.

"Shut up nigga!" she slurred "How you gon' give me the shit then try to stop me from using it! Fuck you!" She threw her middle finger up, resting her head on the back of the expensive leather couch, allowing the pipe to slide from her fingertips to the floor.

Terra stared up at the crystal ceiling that had this unique icicle layout Jay had done before he left. The crack that surged through her system had her hallucinating. In her mind, the ceiling was slowly dropping down on her while at the same time; her body began to climax. Too weak to make out where the feeling was coming from, she took a deep breath and enjoyed her high.

Terra wouldn't have suspected Nicolas of being the one responsible for her body climaxing multiple times. And if she were to ever find out, she would have killed herself.

Nicolas pursued Terra for one reason only. He felt since he couldn't go all the way with the ten year old, he might as well finish where he left off with her mother.

Nicolas didn't have to struggle to get what he wanted. She was high, stretched out on the sofa, and was only wearing Jay's designer robe. Nicolas pulled her hips to the edge of the sofa, dropped to his knees and devoured her wet warmth. Terra moaned out Jay's name enjoying a feverish deep feeling of pleasure. If Terra only knew that the same tongue that had her screaming Jay's name, was the same tongue that had just left her daughter's small cuddle...

Nicolas lived in his own world of sickness and psychotic beliefs. He felt as long as he was in control, Terra and Kemora would never escape his prison of treason and insanity.

*****

"Kemora? Why aren't you eating your breakfast?" Terra asked.

She was running the faucet over the sink rinsing the yellow contents from under her nails where the drugs had stained.

"I'm not hungry Mommy." Kemora rested her chin on the counter.

"Are you sick?" Terra walked toward her feeling her forehead.

"No, and your hand is wet! EWWW!" Kemora wiped the water off her forehead with her sleeve.

"You don't have to go to school today if you don't want to. You can stay home with Mommy." Terra stared into Kemora's eyes. She noticed something was bothering her child but she was too wrapped up in her own problems to pursue her any further.

"The bus is here! Bye Mom!"

Kemora had this all of a sudden burst of energy, dashing out the door!

Kemora? Not wanting to stay home from school? Something's not right; Terra thought as she bit down on her badly need of a manicure nails, watching her daughter get on the bus.

"Hey you."

"Boy, you scared the shit out of me, sneaking up on me like that!" Nicolas towered over her.

"What do you want me to do with this?" He held out the remains of drugs he had given

7

her last night. She stared heavily at them in the small plastic baggies.

"I…I don't think I should this early." She never took her eyes away from the contents that stared back at her.

"Oookay.." He sighed. He knew she couldn't resist.

"Give it here. I might finish them up later."

"It's all good, Terra. There's plenty where that came from." He passed them to her. "Listen, I heard you ask Kemora was something wrong. Is she okay?" He tried to sound concerned.

"She's okay. I just thought she wasn't feeling well. She hasn't been the same since Jay left us. Neither one of us have."

"Yeah, I feel you. I miss that nigga too. I promised him I would never leave y'all hangin'. I'll always be here for you Terra. That's my word."

For the first time, Terra saw something in his eyes that wasn't sincere.

Terra knew she had to bounce back, if not for her, for Kemora's sake. She didn't want to risk losing her child. And if her sister Irene was to ever find out she was using drugs, she would never forgive her.

Since Terra and Jay's mother passed over a year ago, Irene was the only family left on her side. Irene lives in Arizona thousands of miles away. So with that being Terra's least concern, Kemora would be more important to her now. Well, maybe not right at that very moment. Terra had some unfinished smoking to do. She told herself, after finishing off what was left, she wouldn't touch another rock. Terra didn't understand that this kind of failing commitment was common for drug users. Once the drugs were gone, the need and want for more would reappear, and the promise to stop would repeat itself over and over again. It's a revolving door.

Nicolas stood in Terra's bedroom doorway watching her use. He found some kind of sexual inspiration in Terra's self-destructing behavior.

While standing there watching Terra smoke, his mind drifted off thinking about how he'd always wanted Jay's family to one day claim as his own. Nicolas envied Jay's life with Terra and Kemora. He hated watching all the love that surrounded Jay and his family. Once Jay got arrested, Nicolas silently vowed to turn Terra's life into a nightmare. He was fully aware of the consequences if Jay or anyone ever found out about his involvement with Kemora. So, to ensure secrecy, Nicolas instilled fear in Kemora to keep her quiet until she was able to understand *his* kind of love for her.

*****

Kemora was not awake for the last couple of days Nicolas came into her room. He was becoming paranoid because this was not like her. In his own fixated mind, he felt that her being awake when he entered her room was her way of inviting him inside of her solitude. He made an attempt to wake her but, the more he shook her, the louder her snores became. He felt rejected, angry!

One night, after being rejected, he went to the basement where Terra was getting high again. He brought her home some new stuff to try out and she obliged. By the time he made it to Terra, she was out. Nicolas needed to release his frustrations immediately, and once again, he took advantage of her. She was lying in her usual spot; the easy access position. He pulled her thin-laced bikini strap to the side, staring at the rich fur that covered her flesh. Nicolas hungered for its taste again. He slowly opened Terra's thighs, pulling her vaginal lips apart, and then slid his tongue inside of her causing her to squirm.

"Mmmm…" He crooned from the taste that tickled his palette.

Nicolas strained to push his tongue as

deep as he could inside of Terra to gather more of her sweetness, but his tongue couldn't reach the depths of her vagina like his flesh could have. Her moans turned to croons of a sensation that were stimulated by the cocaine that flooded her system. Nicolas had to feel himself inside of her! His flesh was so hard from the foreplay, jacking off couldn't give him the full benefit he desired from her. His only worry was her noticing she had been violated. He couldn't afford that. But apprehension didn't stop him.

"Fuck that…I'm 'bout to do this. Her high ass would probably think the drugs made her feel strange." He mumbled, climbing on top of her, preparing to go on a ride of a lifetime.

Terra hadn't had sex with any other man since Jay. The only other love ever to touch her soul was her crack pipe, so she thought. How naïve to believe…

As Nicolas slid his hardness inside of her, Terra was so high; she couldn't feel the pressure of her walls stretching apart. He tried to be gentle, stroking what felt to him like a warm suction device. That was one thing about cocaine. It was known to raise the body temperature. Between that and her untouched vagina, the feeling to him was almost as good as his fantasy to have sex with ten-year old

Kemora. Nicolas never penetrated Kemora because he knew that would have exposed him if Terra were to ever discover it. None of that changed the fact that his only desire was to have sex with her one day. In a world of his own, he felt as long as he could perform oral sex on Kemora, waiting till she reached the age of 14 would have been well worth it.

*****

Nicolas lost himself inside of Terra, imaging she was Kemora. It made him become more aroused and comfortable within his stokes.

Terra was into the feeling that collided with her high. Again, she thought it was Jay, stretching her vaginal walls with his large penis. She was locked inside a figment of her imagination, daring any man to challenge her pussy to a fight! She began taking control, pulling him into the essence of her soul. Terra opened her thighs, pulling them back so far her knees touched her ears, begging for more. Nicolas watched her. He fell into a trance as he listened to her croons that reminded him an emotional song. She continued to call out the name of the one he envied for years. As he moved in and out of her slowly, he wanted to come. He tried to hold back, brushing his tongue across her black cherry nipples, and then kissing her neck, but the focus was still on his nut that was almost at its peak. That's when Terra locked her legs together around his waist. He tried to break loose of her hold, but she had him sheltered inside of her. The more he attempted to pull away, the more she moved in his direction, swallowing every inch of his flesh.

"Where you goin' Jay?" She aggressively moaned out.

It was too late for Nicolas. He couldn't hold back. Streams of sperm swam deeply into the neglected womb. Nicolas had to think fast! He jumped up, racing up the steps to Terra's private bath to find a douche!

"I can't get you pregnant! Kemora would never forgive me if I did!" Nicolas insanely whispered.

He grabbed all he could and ran back down the steps to Terra before she came around! He placed a towel under her and pushed the semi cool water inside of her, flushing as much semen as he could from her vagina. Terra felt a little discomfort but didn't move nor react. Nicolas proceeded to cleaning her up, and then left her the way he found her.

*****

The following morning was too quiet for

Nicolas. He woke up, looking around the house for Terra and Kemora like nothing happened last night.

"Terra!" Nicolas yelled through the empty space. It was obvious after calling out to her a few times; no one was in the home.   .

The phone rang startling him from the unexpected noise.

"Hello."

"Nick!"

It was Jay

"Hey Man! What's up?"

"Where's my wife playa?"

"I don't know Jay! I just woke up." He yawned.

"Get cho lazy ass up, Boy!!! You supposed to be the man of the house. Where's my baby girl?"

"I told you I haven't seen them this morning. I just woke up and they ain't here." Nicolas said irritated by the sound of Jay's voice. *How this nigga gon' come callin' my family after all this time?* He silently snapped.

"Well, check this out."

"Hold up Jay! I hear keys man."

"What's up Nicolas? Who are you talking to?" Terra asked.

Her speaking to him confirmed she knew nothing about last night.

She was carrying grocery bags as Kemora rushed past them making her way to the bathroom. She didn't speak to Nicolas.

Don't be mad at me baby. I tried to wake you last night... Nicolas thought, noticing Kemora's silence. He felt she was upset with him for not being with her the last few nights.

"NICOLAS!" Terra snapped him out of it!

"Oh! My bad! Telephone... it's Jay."

"HI Baby!" She happily said as she took the phone from Nicolas.

Terra and Jay talked for a while then she gave Kemora the phone to say a few warm words before they hung up.

Terra put up the groceries and then called out to Nicolas.

"Nicolas!"

"Yeah."

"I need to talk to you."

He walked down the steps absent from everything, but a towel that covered his bottom half.

"Where are your clothes?" Terra snapped.

"You called me as I was about to get in the shower. What you expect a nigga to do? It sounded urgent." He stood comfortably in front of her.

Kemora walked in the kitchen while they were talking. Nicolas turned his attention to her, making Terra feel uneasy by the way he winked at Kemora.

"Kemora. Go play. I have to talk to Nicolas." She didn't respond she just quietly walked away.

"What's up?"

"I want you to find another place to stay. I need my space. My life has not been right since Jay left. You've been very supportive Nicolas, and I appreciate everything you've done for Kemora and me, but I can manage on my own now."

Nicolas did not agree with that idea. In fact, unknowingly to Terra, she pushed herself into an early grave. Nicolas kind of felt Jay may have been the one behind her decision. But, if it meant getting rid of Terra, to have Kemora all to himself, she was as good as gone.

Nicolas made Terra feel like he was okay with her decision and moved forward with Plan D... *Death*. She truly had no idea what kind of man she was sharing her space with.

Days went by and Nicolas continued to play up this façade, falsifying documents and information to make it look like he had found a place to live. He had Terra thinking his apartment would have been ready in a few days, which bought him all the time needed to get rid of her. He even went as far as trying to offer her more drugs. She refused them each time. It was hard, but she was determined to try and get herself together.

The last conversation Terra had with Jay depressed her. He told her someone had seen her out at Lee Beauty Supply looking a mess. Not only was Terra embarrassed, she didn't want Jay finding out the real reason behind drugs overruling her appearance.

Right after that phone call she had with Jay; Terra immediately started to make drastic changes in her life. Nicolas just happened to be the first person on her list.

Jay was happy to talk to his family after being in isolation for over 6 months for fighting. Him loosing his privileges over that amount of time effected Kemora, he thought. He tried to explain his reason for not calling, but she was too depressed and disappointed to find room to forgive him. She blamed Jay for leaving them and not being around to protect her from Nicolas' sexual abuse.

Kemora cried when she heard Jay's voice. She wanted to tell him about Nicolas so badly, but she knew that would have been dangerous. She didn't want to risk never seeing him or her mother again, so she shut down. Jay rubbed it off, assuming his little girl was just missing him and made a promise to do all he could to get home to them.

*****

Nicolas knew he couldn't keep prolonging this situation. He had to make a move on Terra before she caught wind of his plot. She had become rude with him and her tolerance level was darn near zero. He was beginning to think she knew something and wasn't telling him. His paranoia was getting the best of him. So within an hour before Kemora would have returned home from school, Terra's body would be tightly wrapped in plastic, waiting to be thrown into the bottom of a Michigan lake. He just simply had to make her disappear.

Nicolas couldn't risk losing Kemora. He was in love with her and that was all he needed to follow through with killing her mother. He knew without Terra around, he would be the next person in line to care for Kemora, and Jay would see to that, he was sure of it. The problem with all of this was... Nicolas truly believed what he was telling himself.

*****

Terra had just gotten out of the shower. The house seemed a little too quiet. But that was because she wasn't high. Crack had her hearing cars miles away, conversations in other homes, flies roaming and bees buzzing. Her ears were extremely sensitive when she was using.

She kind of chuckled at herself as she dried off in front of the mirror. She always wanted to loose a few pounds, but never as much as she did. For the first time she saw where her life was headed. If she hadn't talked to Jay when she did there was no telling where her life would have ended up...without her daughter.

*****

Nicolas twisted the ropes together tightly. He placed some black plastic bags together to cover Terra's body after he killed her. He was only minutes away from Terra when the door bell rung.

"Saved by the bell", he mumbled.

He tiptoed over, peeking through the curtains, noticing a woman and a male officer standing on the other side. The first thing he thought was something had happened to Jay.

Nicolas tossed the rope behind the couch and answered the door.

"Yes."

"Is Miss Cunningham in?"

"Uhh....yes. Let me get her for you."

Nicolas pushed the door up, not inviting them

inside, taking two steps at a time up to Terra's bedroom. She was fully dressed by then.

"The police are at the door, Terra! Go see what they want."

Terra ran down the steps, heart racing, not knowing what to expect!

"I think it's about Jay!" He yelled behind her.

"Yes!" She pulled the door open, breathing hard, waiting for a response.

"We need you to come with us please."

"OH MY GOD! IS IT JAY?" she cried. The officers stared at each other in awe.

"Just come with us."

Terra was arrested once they made it to the station for child abuse and neglect. It seemed that Kemora revealed what Nicolas was doing to her to another child that was also being molested by her grandfather. These two children confided in each other in the school's library. One of the librarians overheard them talking and reported it to the authorities. They later found, after speaking with Terra, who this Nicolas person was and immediately had him picked up.

*****

Terra sat in the courtroom waiting for the judge to pass down sentencing. She was enraged and confused. She blamed herself for not seeing what Nicolas was doing to her child. The judge showed no sympathy toward her. He felt if Terra hadn't been using drugs; she wouldn't have been so careless as to allow any man to take advantage of her child. He didn't hesitate giving her 3 to 15 years in a state prison for 'neglect of a minor child'.

Nicolas received 8 years to life and was later shipped to a penitentiary in Maryland.

Once Jay got wind of what had taken place with his daughter, he immediately got in touch with some of his connects in another penitentiary and had Nicolas killed two months after his incarceration. The autopsy showed Nicolas had been raped and beaten to death.

Kemora went to live with Terra's sister, Irene. Irene had no children and was raising Kemora to the best of her ability. Kemora received counseling and all the love and attention Irene could offer to a child that had been through hell.

When all Terra's test results came back from intake, she was shocked to find her pregnancy test showed up positive. She knew she hadn't been involved with any one since Jay. She was at a total loss. When she thought back to all the evidence indicating foul play left around her coming down off of her high, it

dawned on her...
        Oh my God....Nicolas.

Brave Heart

"Courage have saved many souls young and old…"

*****

"This is how we're going to do this Tavaris. Jason's plane lands at 4:00 pm tomorrow. He usually stops over and visits his Mom before he makes his way over here to see his rug rats that he left me with. That's when you can come in and do your thing!" Roberta plotted with her baby's father, Tavaris.

"That's a bet. Now, check this out Baby Girl. I'm gon' holla at my man DT about some weapons, and I'll be back around five tomorrow to rap things up. I'm gon' be nice and give this fool a little time to chill with his monkeys. That nigga think I'm stupid! He don't give a fuck about them boys Roberta! I know that fool just be fallin' through here cause he think you gon' give 'em some ass!" Tavaris said, jealously as he walked out of the front door.

Roberta has three children. A two year-old daughter named Ashley, by Tavaris, a neighborhood thug that could care less about anyone other than his seed. And two sons by Jason named Jason Jr., a seven year-old and

Jaru, who is nine.

Jason is an older, mature man that takes good care of his boys. Jason Jr. and Jaru are very well mannered children, never causing problems for anyone. On the other hand, her daughter, Ashley is rotten to the core.

Roberta has no tolerance when it comes to her two boys. And her attitude and lack of respect for herself runs her life. Roberta allows Tavaris to beat on her sons and sometimes leaves bruises and scars. He hates the fact that Roberta has kids by another man and it's not going to be long before he comes up with a malicious plot to get rid of them. But, right now his only focus was finding a way to pull together enough money to handle a long overdue debt that has his life at stake.

Tavaris owed some local drug dealers in the neighborhood a substantial amount of money for drugs he misused. With very little time and limited sources, Roberta's idea to take out her sons' father, Jason, came just in time for Tavaris. Jason was worth a half of million dollars alive and double the amount dead. Due to the fact that Roberta never cared about anyone but herself, taking out her son's father, for money was easy. It's just sad that Jason and her two boys would have to be the ones to suffer in the end.

Jason looked forward to being with his sons every time he came to town. His original plan was to take custody of them and place them in a safe environment where they would be able to experience good living and attend private schools. Jason sent Roberta more than three thousand dollars every month. He just wanted to take good care of the mother of his two boys. He knew there was no other way around it; he wasn't in the home. Plus he knew she could use the extra cash to help with the new member in the family. Jason was always fair and tried to support Roberta in all ways possible.

He used to do more until she chose what he called a *bum* as her man. Then when she got pregnant, not only was he hurt, he knew the relationship between them was over. Either way, he continued to take care of his responsibilities; doing the best he could for her until he was able to remove his sons from under her roof...for good.

Jason had a business set up overseas that was starting to take off. With that going for himself, he was planning to seek custody rights on this trip. Just like anyone else that was unaware of his or her life expectancy, Jason never saw his last day coming. He knew from experience that Roberta wasn't dealing with a full deck, but he would have never thought she would have set him up to be killed.

Jason Jr. and Jaru waited anxiously for their dad to return. As they stared from their bedroom window, Roberta held on to Ashley, trying to rock her to sleep. She didn't want her baby to witness such a horrific murder and this was the only way she knew how to avoid exposing her daughter to violence.

The doorbell rang and there was Jason. He was standing there anxiously anticipating his visit with his sons.

"Jason Jr.! Jaru!! Get down here!!" Roberta yelled up the steps for the boys to come down to see their father.

"Here we come Ma!" they responded excitedly.

They both leaped down the steps, jumping into their father's arms. Jason Jr. was so overjoyed that he forgot about the severe beating he had just received from Tavaris a couple of days ago that left painful bruises on his back. By the time he realized it; it was too late.

When Jason took hold of them, Jason Jr. squirmed in pain. Jason slowly lowered them to the floor focusing on Jason Jr., asking him what was wrong. Roberta was standing behind Jason facing the boys. She made sure they saw her evil glare that let them know they had better not say a word. They got the message. Jaru came up with one of his usual school explanations whenever his teacher would ask him the same question about the bruises she would see on him from time to time. He told his dad that they were playing in the yard and Jason Jr. got hurt. Jason believed Jaru and off to the living room they went. Roberta made her way to the kitchen with little Ashley attached at her hip.

This nigga better hurry up! What the hell is taking him so damned long?

She peeked out the side of her kitchen window and there Tavaris sat in an old beat up Chevy, placing a mask over his head, preparing for the ambush. Roberta started to feel chills and she pulled the baby closer to her. She knew it was too late to turn back. The only thing she could do at this point was get a grip and let the dice roll.

"Now… How old are you Jason Jr..?" Jason sat on the floor with Jason Jr.. on his lap.

"I'm seven, Daddy." He giggled showing his two missing front teeth.

"Ooookay." He tapped his nose and turned to Jaru and asked, "And how old are you now, big fella?"

"Old enough to have a girlfriend."

They all laughed and started to wrestle on the floor. This just made things harder on Roberta. She knew after this tragedy it was going to take a lot of counseling, time and energy to pull her sons back together.

She started biting her nails and trembling non-stop until a voice startled her from the front room.

"ROBERTA!!! GET IN HERE NOW!!"

She rushed into the living room where she faced an irate man that was holding up the shirt of Jason Jr.. exposing the bruises that covered his small back. She instantly became frantic.

"What...the fuck...is this Roberta???"

Before she could say a word her front door flew off the hinges! There was complete chaos! Jason Jr. was clinging onto his daddy's leg as Jaru flew up the steps scared for his life! Roberta tried to snatch Jason Jr.. from his grip on his father but he wouldn't let go. He was determined to hold on to the only one he trusted. Roberta couldn't calm Ashley down so she tried to muffle her cries through all the commotion.

"I want your money and them muthafuckin' keys to that nice ride outside, NOW!!" the man behind the mask demanded with an AK pointed in Jason's face.

"Please son, put the gun down. You can have what ever you want. Just don't hurt my family."

That set off a rage in Tavaris' head.

Your family? He said to himself.

Tavaris drew back the gun and kicked Jason in the chest, knocking him against the fireplace! Jason Jr. almost fell back, but through it all little man didn't lose his grip. Those little small tiny fingers held on for dear life. Tavaris took the handle of his gun and started beating Jason in his head profusely. Roberta screamed for him to stop and made an attempt to pull him off of Jason. Tavaris calmed down a little, shook it off and said,

"Don't you say one muthafuckin' word bitch! Get yo' punk ass up and give me what I asked for!"

He aimed the gun at Jason's chest as he struggled through pain to pull his wallet from his pocket along with the keys.

Jason Jr.. was in shock crying uncontrollably, "Don't hurt my daddy pleeeease!!!"

Tavaris glanced over at Jason Jr.. making eye contact through the cut out circles on his mask. That was one thing Jason Jr. could never forget...those evil eyes of Tavaris. He witnessed those eyes every time he would beat on him and his brother. But before Jason Jr.. could utter the words from his lips to warn his daddy who the face was behind the mask, Tavaris raised the gun and said,

"Fuck you bitch! You took too long."

The only thing that graced the room was gunshots and bullets claiming souls. Blood and flesh splattered on loved ones while heart rates were rising and falling. It was over. Jason fell back against the floor with Jason Jr.. holding him tightly. Roberta sat the whining baby on the sofa chair. She dropped to the floor next to Tavaris crying. "OH MY GOD TAVARIS!!!" Roberta cried out before pulling his mask away. Never once did Roberta notice that what she was saying confirmed that she knew.

Jason stared at her in disbelief saying to himself, *how did she know who this man was???*

Jason placed his thought on hold while he made his way over to his son, Jaru. He was still holding a .357 at the bottom of the steps. If it hadn't been for the courage of a nine year old, his father would be dead.

"Give me the gun son." Jason eased up on Jaru and gently pulled the gun from his hands.

Jaru fell into his father's arms; releasing

all the pain that he'd been hiding from him for the last two years.

Once the police came and gathered up all the evidence along with Tavaris' dead body, everything came out. Roberta's plot to take Jason out was exposed. She wasn't the one who admitted it. Jaru told everything. He overheard her talking to Tavaris about the scheme and he was able to make a statement against his mother. That was one thing about Roberta and Tavaris were very careless about...her children. Jaru witnessed Tavaris placing his gun under his mom's mattress many times so he knew where the heat was hidden. Roberta had no respect for her children. It was so bad that she would have sex in front of them when they were young but old enough to know what was going on. She would freely disclose her personal business around them; not realizing that kids have more sense than some grown folks in the world today.

Roberta ended up losing custody of all of her children and receiving a sentence of twenty-five years to life in prison.

Tavaris didn't have any family so Ashley had to go live with Roberta's family who couldn't stand Tavaris or his rotten child. They noticed how Roberta showed favoritism among her children and they always imagined taking control over the situation. They just never knew the opportunity would come under these circumstances.

Jaru and Jason Jr.. are now in private school and living in a beautiful home overseas. They have everything they want...life for them is complete.

Jason always reassured them that whenever they wanted to go visit their mom they could. But they decided it was best if they wrote her out of their lives for the time being. They needed time to allow the healing process to begin. Later, if they felt their mom deserved to be a part of their lives they would decide whether or not to see her again.

Jason continued to send money home to Roberta's family to assist with the care of Ashley. He felt that in spite of what happened, she was still just an innocent child who had no control over her situation.

Jason upholds his position as a man with integrity and morals. He will always continue to be what men in the world should be...responsible men...

Things About Her Life She Wouldn't Tell a Priest

"Shhhhh...the best secret is within you..."

D'Norah

Society doesn't understand me and sometimes I wonder if God ever loved me. As a child I'd experienced all the worst things in life. I don't even know where to begin. I hear many say everyone has a story to tell but I still believe mine was only one of a kind.

Abuse and incest were some of the minor things I witnessed and experienced. How about catching your mother and father having sex with your seventeen year old sister? I admit my sister was wild, but I never knew how wild until the first time I walked in on them all in bed together. I thought I would fall out and die right before their eyes. Mom instantly jumped out the bed, rushing toward me as Dad pulled a sheet over his and my sister's naked body! I wanted to believe that what I had just seen was a nightmare and when I woke up Dad would be the only one in the bed with Mom. It wasn't a nightmare and it was just the beginning of mine.

My parents never married and the only time I would see my dad was when Mom was throwing sex parties or they were having their own. I'm willing to bet there weren't many sick families on this planet that had witnessed such evilness under one roof. So, like I said earlier... my family... was one of a kind.

We all had our share of laughter, but it was only when there was something good on T.V. Other than that, my Dad and Mom always had something wild and crazy up their sleeves. I would pray the day would never come when my mom would invite me into their sick sexual solitude. At one point I had become worried about my sister's welfare. But after watching her behavior and noticing how she had become this different person, I knew trouble was soon to follow. It was like she looked forward to their invitation. I noticed how she had become Dad's favorite and it wasn't long before my mother was sleeping on the couch.

As much as I didn't want to accept the world I was born into, it took me years to realize I had no choice. None of my siblings stuck together and it was every man for himself in our home. If our friends would come by, we had to pretend to be normal. If other family members would come over, we had to act fake. We were playing roles and didn't even practice for the parts.

Out of this confused childhood I lived in, I just wanted to be something different. I didn't want to be like anyone I knew. I wanted to be something of a different world, a planet that took millions of years to get to. I wanted to be somewhere far away, nonexistence. This is the world I moved to, at a very early stage in my life, leaving behind my family and making moves toward finding new friends...

All Grown Up

I'm a lesbian...I think. I have been with several women, never falling deep enough to give myself to them completely. I question my childhood hoping to find the answer. Why am I confused about my sexual preference? I could say it was from many things that happened during the wonder years but either way it doesn't matter now. I like aggressive women with a manly touch and sex appeal. Men have had the opportunity to see how good this pussy was too, but there was something about the way women treated it that got the respect they demanded.

I'm still confused though. It's like I'm

going through a phase. I can go back as far as my first orgasm. Believe it or not it was with a kitten. I had this kitten named Sheila that I forced to stroke my clit with her tongue. How I got her to do it was still a mystery, but it was some bomb ass cat-head fo'sho! I was just experimenting being that everyone in my home was having sex.

My first just happened to be with a cat. I had to have run through at least three cats as far as I can remember. Two of them were killed by my other siblings and the other went out my bedroom window after it bit the tip of my clit. My mom wasn't having no more cats in our home so I had to move on to bigger and better things.

The next just happened to be my cousin Althea. She was from Florida. They would all come up for the summer and Althea and I would do our thang. She played with my tits while she thought I was asleep. I was so into the way she sucked my nipples that my body looked forward to her touch every night. The feeling of her thinking I was asleep made it even more interesting. One night I purposely removed my panties before getting in the bed and just like I thought, she played with my pussy. It was one of the best orgasms I'd had since my cats. As she was touring my vagina with her tongue I couldn't help but to rotate my hips to meet her every move. I think maybe if she had been a guy, men might be more of my choice today. But, it doesn't matter. I'm just living my life and enjoying sex while I'm still young.

Threesome

I met this guy named Duan through this girl that reminded me of my brother Jay and I was instantly attracted to him. It's been over 10 years since I'd last seen my family. Last I heard, Mom left Dad for a woman, my Dad was still doing what he does best, fuck, and my pitiful sister was still obsessed with him.

Dad was this young, arrogant, pretty-boy that got his way whether he was right or wrong. My mother, on the other hand, was naïve. She knew Dad had a sexual desire and he'd do almost anything to keep things interesting. I was just shocked that she would go as far as using her own child as one of their sex toys. Either way, I don't miss none of their asses at all and I'm on some new shit! This Jay look-alike got me horny as hell. I didn't know whether these feelings for this guy were coming from all the incest in my family or what. But I do know this, I'm givin' him and his girl the pussy tonight.

A Week After The Threesome

I'm pregnant and I wanted to have an abortion. I talked it over with Duan and his girlfriend and they both turned their backs on me... claiming the baby wasn't his. I know I'm not ready for a child but just to be vindictive, I chose to have it anyway. A little boy.

Duan was a bum and I knew it when I fucked him. I don't know why I didn't insist on using some kind of protection. I was weak when it came to that. It didn't matter either way because I loved my baby and we didn't need him.

My son was the king of my throne. I had this different kind of love for him. It was a strange kind of love that no one but me would ever understand. At one time I was afraid he would be gay by there being no male figure in his life. He would play with some of my friends' kids and their baby dolls instead of his own toys. He would walk around the house with my heels on and when kids asked him what he wanted to be when he grew up, he surprisingly placed his hand on his hip and said, "I want to be Beyonce!" I didn't know whether to beat his ass or cry. I knew then something had to be done. I felt I had no other choice other than to expose him to my wild side.

6

He was very smart for a two year old. He talked better than some adults. I blamed his knowledge on these vitamins I took while I was carrying him called *Gingko Bilbo*. This boy walked before he crawled and talked more than he cried. I knew I had a little man in a child's body.

Anyway, like I was saying about the gay thing, I didn't want him to grow up to be no fag so I had to do what I felt I could do, as his mother, to protect him. I allowed him to watch porno movies and I would invite some of my male associates over and have sex in front of him. Some of them would question what I was doing and others found it interesting. This was my way of raising a man and I truly believed it was my right.

Now He Wants to Come Back

Duan came knocking at my door one day saying he left his girlfriend for cheating on him. I gave him a hard time at first, but I ended up letting him back in. You would never guess what he brought me as a gift of his apology…a damn cat! I thought that was strange and the more he was around us, the stranger he became.

Our son had a hard time adapting to him. He was so used to just me and him in the house that he wasn't at all prepared for no man moving in our space...father or not. My baby had become rebellious, cursing and yelling, that Duan spanked him a few times. I couldn't deal with him hitting my son and tried to stop him but he ignored me, throwing his strap across my ass, causing my skin to bruise. Duan said I spoiled my son, allowing him to disrespect adults and run my household...he just didn't know the kind of bond my son and I shared.

The longer he lived with us, the more unhappy I was. I started hating him. He didn't allow our son in the same room with us during sex. And he questioned me about our son's persistence and anger when he would put him out. Duan never noticed him sneaking back into the room once to watch us. This one time in particular I purposely pulled the covers off of us when I noticed him peaking around the corner. My intensions were for him to receive the full benefit of a man and woman having sex. That was until Duan got out of control in the way he was handling me. That was the first time and the last time my son was exposed to me and Duan having sex after that.

Duan loved rough sex. He did all kinds of things to my body. Sometimes it would be so painful that I would have to fight my way out of it. That always seemed to make things worse. I'll never forget the time Duan was upset with me for something I said. Shortly after that we had sex and I paid for it dearly. He sucked on my left nipple so hard and long, I cried in pain. He didn't budge or come up for air. It was like he was hungering for something inside of my breast. He had to have stayed on that one nipple for fifteen minutes or more. I was paralyzed. I didn't know whether the pain was from that or the fact the he had his whole hand inside of me. There was never a time we had sex that I didn't bleed afterwards. Many times I would try to push him away but he became more aggressive and persistent. He had my arms pinned over my head and my cherry stretched from Detroit to Lansing. He was a sex maniac that loved to see people in pain.

Sometimes I dreaded doing it with him. But every time I would say no, he would basically rape me. It was like rejection turned him on.

I never knew what anal sex was until now. I tried not to scream the night he went up in my behind. He didn't consider using no kind of lubrication other than the saliva that came from him brushing his tongue across my anal. I never expected what he had in store for me because the feeling of him lickin' my ass felt good. But when he slid his flesh in me I screamed so loudly, I just knew other tenants in my building had to have heard me! He had made an attempt to cover my mouth and I bit him, trying my best to get him off of me. He laughed, applying more pressure, forcing himself deeper into my tight soul, calling me his bitch, his whore, and other degrading names. I felt cheap. I cried and begged him to stop. He ignored me, forcing me into an even more uncomfortable position. I made another attempt to scratch him and he grabbed the head board using all the strength he had to pull himself even deeper into me. He damn near lifted me off the bed, almost standing to his feet! His moans and groans revealed a sexual tension being released from years of pain and torture to a person scorned. And even all of that wasn't enough for him. He kept his pace, lowering my knees back to the mattress. Then he spread my thighs so wide I felt them crack. Finally, like a snake, he slithered his hand around my waist placing at least four of his fingers all the way inside of my vagina while his other hand still held on to the headboard. He had both entrances of my body locked and under his control. I couldn't do anything but take it. I couldn't fight him. He was too strong and I was too tired.

I just stopped screaming and laid there like *Nettie* in *"The Color Purple"*. I was officially his sex toy.

A knock At My Door

Some days when he would go out, I contemplated taking my son and running away. But I had no where to go. I felt stuck, trapped, like I was being held hostage in my own home. Then one day when Duan wasn't home a nightmare from my past came knocking at my door. The visit was both unexpected and unwanted. It was then when I came face to face with a life I tried to bury the day I walked out of my family's home.

Side Swiped

"The things you can't communicate will run your life"

*****

"So you mean to tell me I'm going to die? I can't die like this! What the hell am I supposed to do now?" Farrah cried out to her gynecologist after receiving her HIV results.

"Farrah, please listen to me. I realize this is hard for you to accept right now, but HIV is not a death sentence. There are many new medications and treatments to help you get through this. I come across many people in your situation that live long healthy lives with this virus. You can..."

"FUCK YOU AND YOUR ADVICE!!" She jumped up out of the chair and ran out of her doctor's office hysterically. The only thing she could think of at that point was suicide.

Dr. Kym Rapaulzi was used to seeing this kind of reaction when dealing with situations like this. She felt HIV was running rampant with women as young as Farrah. And witnessing the way this virus is dominating today's women, men and children made it even harder to cope

1

with.

*****

Farrah's head was spinning as she jumped into her Ford Five Hundred. Her boyfriend, Roland, had just purchased it for her last week. At first she felt he could have been the one held responsible for what had just happened to her, but then again, maybe not.

Farrah and Roland had been living together for the last couple of years and during that time they both tested negative for HIV. So that left one other thing; the gang rape that went down a couple of months ago. She tried to place it behind her, but now it was harder than ever.

Farrah had been dancing at this local strip bar for the last seven years off 8 Mile in Detroit. One night a couple of regulars swung by and gave her an offer she couldn't refuse. Farrah admits she was a little tipsy when the offer was made and that alone could have clouded her judgment. Nevertheless, when it came to that all mighty dollar, Farrah didn't waste any time making it. The agreement was that she would be cashed out to dance for them at an exclusive hotel after she got off work.

Farrah thought, *"Humm... It's only three of them. I can handle that."*

After work, she left with dude and two of his boys ready to make that paper to take home and share with her Boo. The whole ride over there, Farrah never suspected anything. It wasn't until she walked through the door of the hotel room and saw over ten hungry, drunk, fools anxiously awaiting some action. There was no turning back. Before she could get in the door good, they were all over her. It was like mating season for wild animals. They didn't care anything about their raw flesh touching another's! It was all about the kill. Farrah tried to blame some of the things she had seen going on around her on ecstasy pills and way too many drinks.

As the pain increased and the lights became brighter she realized the men were in fact screwing each other!!! It was wild! There were at least two or three on her at one time. She felt herself dying a slow death as they violated every open space on her body. All the deep groans and moans started to fade and then she blacked out. She awakened naked, and in a puddle of semen. She could barely walk. She held onto anything in her reach to pull herself up off the floor.

Farrah knew she couldn't face Roland right now. She disappeared for about two weeks. That gave her more than enough time to heal. Roland figured that she had run off with one of her tricks from the bar. The thought of her doing him this way set off a rage that wanted nothing but revenge. But as the days grew longer, he became worried. Before he could make a police report, she appeared like nothing had happened. He was so furious that he jumped on her beating her into a new day. Farrah felt she deserved every blow to the head and made no attempt to fight him back.

Shortly after that, Roland took all of his anger out on the pussy. He devoured her, head first—in between her thighs.

If he only knew how many dicks he was sucking on he would kill me, Farrah thought silently as she enjoyed the feeling of having make-up sex with her man.

*****

Farrah lay in the dark trying to gather her thoughts. This was critical thinking time for her. She sat staring at the bottle of Tylenol 4's on her dresser.

If I kill myself I won't have to die slowly. But, if I live and try to work this thing out, they might end up finding a cure…or maybe not. I don't know what to do or how to handle this. How will I tell Roland? I can't. I can't tell him this. He will leave me. Hell! He will probably kill me! I need to go away and think. That's what I'll do. Go away...and think.

*****

For the last two days Roland had been looking for Farrah. She hadn't called or been home and he was becoming paranoid. The problem with this was not the fact that she was missing. It was why she was missing that concerned him.

Roland wanted to place what was really bothering him in the back of his mind for the time being, but he couldn't. He knew he would have to face this one day. He just never thought it would be this soon.

Farrah told Roland a couple of weeks ago she was taking another HIV test. He accused her of messing around. Otherwise why would she all of a sudden retake the test? Of course she denied his allegations, but he pursued her in an effort to persuade her from not going through with it.

Farrah came up with one her famous lies saying that her boss had been receiving complaints that there were rumors of someone working at his bar that was HIV positive and was spreading it to clients. She said her boss told all the girls to take a mandatory HIV test if they wanted to continue to work for him.

Roland didn't by that story mainly because of his own hidden secret.

His original plan was to go to his grave with what he had been hiding from her for many years, but now, things had changed. Roland knew in his heart that Farrah's HIV results would come back positive. Hell, he was the one responsible for this mishap! Not only has he been involved with a few men over the last four years, he messed around and got caught up with someone who had plans for his soul. Roland fell straight into a trap.

When Farrah first came up with the idea for them to get tested in the early stages of their relationship Roland had a hard time finding the courage to go through with it. But he convinced himself by saying, *"Hell, she's a dancer. If anyone should be scared of taking this test it would be her. Fuck it! I'm gon' die one day anyway."*

When their results came back negative, Roland made a commitment that he would lay low *on the down low*. But all that changed as soon as another *He-She* came through and swept him off of his feet. Like a dope fiend that was trying to say *NO* to drugs, he relapsed. It was then when he felt he had a problem.

One night while hangin' out with his boys he thought, *what is it about these men that makes my dick hard? Hell, Im'a man, Fuck! I love pussy, but I'm one confused muthafucka, I swear! One minute I'm hangin wit' the fellas actin' hard like a nigga wit know issues. And then next, I'm creepin' to run up in a niggas ass. I need some fuckin' counselin'.*

Roland came to the conclusion that being with a man gave him something a woman couldn't. One time he thought about moving away with this *mystery lover*, but his manhood stepped up and claimed its spot. Plus, he couldn't see himself labeled as *GAY*. Every time his *lover* would mention that word in his presence he would disappear for days at a time. He would return to Farrah after being with his male *lover* and make love to her like she was the only one that existed in his world. He made sure there were no doubts or slip-ups when it came to challenging his manhood. All and all, he felt she would have a hard time holding him accountable if she was to turn up HIV positive.

Either way, having to live with his nightmare would be a life long battle and never forgotten. Roland couldn't get past how his *lover* played him. He thought they had real hard love for one another. He would have never suspected betrayal.

One day Roland was having some

problems at home with Farrah and he just wanted to get away for a few days. He knew his *lover* was growing tired of him going back and forth between the two, but he never knew it was at a point where his life was at stake.

Roland was missing his *lover* and decided to pop in on him, so he drove over, unexpectedly, parked his car in the garage and turned the key in the lock to find everything gone, but a note on the counter.

Baby...I don't know how to tell you this, but...I have been HIV positive going on two years now. I wanted to tell you so bad before we had sex, but again, I guess you could say I was being a little vain. A part of me felt alone in a world that selfishly claimed me. I needed someone to share my pain, to feel what I was feeling. I trusted the person who gave this disease to me just as you trusted me when I gave it to you. Don't blame yourself. None of this is your fault. This was planned for you like it was for me. God works in mysterious ways, Roland. We have been taking advantage of Him for so long that I guess He got tired of us. Now it's time to move on to a world that we will soon share together. Please... don't come looking for me. I want to die in peace and that's what I left you to do. My situation has now become serious. My doctors told me I have 3 months left. This may sound cruel but, you made the bed, now we can lie in it together. I can't wait to have you all to myself in a world of our own.

I Love You... See you soon...

After forcing himself to read his death sentence he felt like someone was standing behind him with a gun to his head giving him three seconds before they pulled the trigger. The only thing he could see himself doing at that point was killing that fool before he died on his own. He wanted revenge! He wanted answers! And if it meant going on a world-wide hunt to find the one who stole his dream, well... whatever it would take to make it happen, was his goal.

After coming by everyday hoping to find a piece of mail or any leads of where he may have relocated, Roland ran into an unexpected visitor.

"What up playa?" Roland approached the guy that was heading toward the porch.

"I'm sorry...do I know you?" the guy said to him.

"Who you lookin' for?" Roland ignored the way he was becoming cocky.

"I'm just here to pick up my brother's mail and anything else he may have left behind."

"Oh. I apologize, I didn't...."

"No need. Were you aware that he passed at 6 this morning?"

Roland's heart raced. A part of him felt something, but the other part of him wanted to be the one standing over him when he died. The whole thing took him by surprise. He had been a nervous wreck and it was only a matter of time before everything hit the fan.

"I got to get home to my girl..."

The guy stared at Roland as he jumped into his truck and skirted up the street.

.evol nI looF A

"Sometimes a woman would sacrifice who she is to become something she's not..."

*****

"Monae', you have a call on line one."

"Thank you Marilyn." I finished up my corned beef sandwich and picked up the phone. " Hello?"

"What up gorgeous?"

"Nothing, just finished eating. What's up?"

"You." he responded and then continued with the bull. "I can't wait to see you. I want to make up for last night."

"Last night is behind us Rocky." I said annoyed.

"Let's go to the Star tonight to check out that new flick, damn...what's the name of it?" His mind raced to try and remember.

"Oh! *4 Brothers*, one of the John Singleton movies. You know I don't do the movie thang, but I heard it was tight."

"You're...taking me out? What did I do to deserve this?" I asked, kind of surprised.

"Come on now...you know you good for it." he said in his manipulative voice.

He was so full of it!

1

He continued, "Check this out, did you read those instructions I left for you this morning?"

"Not yet. I've been so busy today. I haven't had any room to do nothing since I got here."

He got quiet. Then his tone moved from warm to cold, "You didn't do what I told you? I'll see you at your crib at 7."

"How you know I will be there at 7?"

"Ohhh, I know. See you at 7." He said with aggressive confidence and he hung up.

I should have expected this phone call wasn't about me and him and no damned movie! I've been around Rocky long enough to know that his only love outside of his mom was his hustle.

This had made leaving him even easier for me now. I'm tired of him using me! When he gets to my place, I have to let him know it's over. I can't take this anymore.

Before I left my office, I had to call my dad. I hadn't talked to him in a while and something had been telling me to make that happen.

Dad never approved of Rocky, and now more than ever I should have upheld the *'Parents Know Best'* rule.

Rocky was complicated. I thought dad

was just tripping because of the way he carried himself. But then again, I had a lot to lose by lowering my standards. Here it was, I had a degree in Psychology and I still couldn't figure him out. It seemed like every time I tried to get inside of his head, he ended up in mine. I just couldn't win for losing. I thought I had control over my emotions, but obviously not. This twenty-seven year old man held the key to my heart...and my home.

I'll never forget the words my dad said to me after meeting Rocky. He said that Rocky was bad news and if I pursued a relationship with him he would be the death of me. And being the 'hard-headed-you-can't-tell-me-nothing' brat that I was, I didn't listen and fell idiotically in love. I gave up my position as daddy's little girl which consisted of trying to meet all of his requirements. Becoming a psychologist was one of my most ultimate tasks!

I needed some excitement in my life and Rocky fulfilled that. I felt like I wasn't getting younger after just turning thirty-seven. I wanted to have children and get married before I turned forty! Now, only a year away from reaching my goal I realized what a foolish mistake I'd made. The only thing I could say to myself was... *"I wish I would have listened to my father..."*

Walking Through the Door of Death...
Monae'

As soon as I walked through the front door of my condo someone snatched me by the neck placing his hand over my mouth! I was so terrified I almost urinated on myself! The man behind the mask kicked the door closed with the heel of his foot and threw me into the wall. I tried to fight to break free, but the struggle was useless. He had such a tight grip on my neck I couldn't break away! He tossed my petite frame from the wall over my living room couch and shushed me. I was distraught! My heart was racing so fast I felt my breath being snatched away! When he eased his hand away from my mouth, my first reaction was to scream as loudly as I could...wrong move! This person commenced to beating me until I damned near fainted!

"BITCH!" he yelled, slapping me to the floor! "WHERE'S THE FUCKING STASH?" He threw his foot against me causing a shortness of breath.

The last kick to my right rib caused me to cough up my food from earlier. I knew I was dead. What scared me the most was the fact that I didn't know what he was talking about!

"PPPlease…" I painfully stammered. "I don't have…" That was all I could get out before he started dragging me through my home by my hair. I was screaming and crying out loud. I tried to hold his wrists to prevent my hair from tearing away from my scalp. He was turning over vases and carelessly knocking over anything in his way! I just knew my life was soon to be over at any given moment.

Surprisingly, he eased up dropping me to the floor. I was scared to look at him. I just wanted someone, anyone to help me! My body was shaking and I could feel his presence near, standing over me. Then I heard his voice, and it was one that I have heard a million times before…*oh my God….*

Rocky

"I don't give a fuck about what y'all niggas is talkin' about! I want my muthafuckin' money!" Rocky demanded over the phone.

He was having a conference call with a few of his business associates that had fallen behind on a transaction.

"Hey, hey…" Rocky intervened while the fellas were talking over each other on his other end, "I ain't got time for this right now! Get at me later!" He ended the call.

Rocky pressed his foot into the accelerator, pushing his black SL 500 through traffic to pick up Monae' before the movie started. He thought about all she had put up with since they'd been together. He kept telling himself he would make it up to her someday, but at that moment, his only focus, outside the business side of their relationship, was making it to the movies before it had become too late. Never once would he have expected a set up that just might put an end to his glamorous life...

Monae'

"MONAE'!" Rocky yelled my name, entering with his key.

Before he could close the door his stepbrother, Kenneth, took him from behind placing a gun against the small of his back, and forced him inside.

"What the fuc...." Rocky made an attempt to say something. "AUHHH F...UCK!!" A sharp pain shot through his head from being struck with the handle of the gun Kenneth was holding! The only thing I could see through my swollen eyes was white meat exposed from the gash on Rocky's head.

"Get'cho punk-ass over there!" Kenneth

demanded as he pushed Rocky into a chair next to the one I was duck taped and tied to. Kenneth aimed the gun at Rocky's head. He could barely hold his head up. I was bleeding so badly. Rocky didn't want to believe that the guy standing before him ready to take his life was the same guy that shared his space for many years.

"Yo..." Rocky lifted his head, staring in Kenneth's eyes. "What the fuck is you doin' man?" He agonizingly forced the words from his mouth.

"You'll see muthafucka!" Kenneth smirked, securing Rocky's wrists behind his back.

Kenneth sent a chirp to his accomplice to inform that he had us under control. Within a few moments I heard my front door open and close. The footsteps that were making their way toward us made me even more uncomfortable. I felt like I was suffering and just waiting for God to call me home.

"I see you finally done somethin' right, Son."

"Son?" I muttered, shocked after noticing all that was involved.

I was almost afraid to look into the eyes of the person behind that familiar voice. I went into total shock at that very moment.

"YOU PUNK ASS BITCHES!!!" Rocky shouted! He tried to struggle and wiggle his way loose from the rope. Rocky knew this was a do or die mission! If he had to die in the process of trying to save our lives, his mind was set.

There was no doubt that his stepbrother, Kenneth, and stepfather, Paul, were going to kill us. Once they found whatever it was they were looking for, it was over. There was no way they would allow us to live after exposing themselves.

"Get cho' ass back, Bitch!" Kenneth kicked Rocky over in his chair. He fell straight on his back still struggling to break loose. Kenneth stood over him aiming the gun and cocking it. I tried to cry out through the tape that covered my mouth. I could see hate and envy in his eyes as he stared down at Rocky. Kenneth was ready to kill.

"NO! Not yet son. We have to find the money first!" Paul yelled to stop him.

"You lucky boy." Kenneth grimmed Rocky.

He grabbed Rocky by the neck of his t-shirt and pulled him back up.

"So what's it going to be step-son?" Paul asked mischievously. Rocky gave him a stare that clearly read: *"Fool, I'm gon' kill your ass if I get out of this! That's what up!*

Rocky turned to me. I could tell he was getting angrier by the second. I could only imagine how bad I looked to him after Kenneth knocked me all over the place. That only added fuel to the fire. I felt like I was suffocating from the tape covering my mouth and the mucus that clogged my nose. I could hardly breathe. My jaw was sore and I was bleeding from my right eye. I was losing my faith.

"I tell you what Big Bro. You could tell us where the stash is and I'll leave the rest up to the man who knocked your mother up and married her." Kenneth smirked. Rocky turned his attention back to the both of them. He looked like he was thinking up a master plan. I was so scared I felt I would die long before the bullet hit my head.

"I can't fuckin' believe that y'all fools would play me and my girl like this, yo! This shit is fucked up!" Kenneth and Paul moved in closer. Rocky had no idea how pressed for time they were.

"Rocky, if I was you, I wouldn't be reminiscing right now, I would be telling these two hungry niggas standing in your face with a gun where the MOTHER FUCKING MONEY IS!" Paul was up in Rocky's face. I could tell

9

from his tone he hated the ground Rocky walked on and the mother that birthed him. He was a very evil man.

Rocky attempted to attack Paul, but Kenneth smacked him across the face with the gun again. This time splattering blood all over me! I freaked out! No one could tell me that I wasn't having a nightmare!

"This is the last time Rocky!" Paul said with vengeance. Rocky was losing all consciousness.

"I-I-I ain't telling y'all SHIT!" He spit blood on the floor and dropped his head. It was then Rocky knew there was nothing he could do to save us. That was one of the things I learned from being with a drug dealer; never give up information in a situation like this no matter what. Either way you look at it it's a kill or be killed environment.

Rocky turned to look at me. I knew in my heart it would be the last time we would see each other in this life. I continued to cry as I felt death approaching. But there was something about what he said to me that gave me sense of peace.

"I'm sorry baby…"

For the first time in our relationship, I knew his apology was genuine. I just hated it had to come to this before he expressed his regret.

Reflecting Back Over Our Lives...
Monae'

The day Rocky and I met...it was under compelling circumstances. I have myself to blame for it. I was unprofessional, naïve, and I deserved what ever came my way, good or bad.

I used to offer pre-martial counseling to couples that was part of an evaluation recommended before marriage through the state.

On a weekly basis, I would give each couple two hours of required time. Out of the few couples I counseled, I took an interest in one in particular, Rocky and his fiancé, Amina. Not only was she just a fool in love. Rocky had issues dealing with commitment and loyalty. They were both too young and not ready to take this to another level.

Amina was an extremely gorgeous woman with no common sense. The more she talked the more aware I had become. Listening to her helped me to determine she hadn't finished high school. She called maggots magnets and co-defendants co-dependents. She talked herself tired and me rich. I made over 14 ½ hours worth of pay listening to her!

On the other hand, Rocky was very handsome, intellectual and flirtatious. During our sessions, I would be trying to focus on what she was saying, while he would be making indirect advances at me behind her back! I realized I was being unprofessional by allowing this type of behavior to continue, but he was turning me on. I was instantly attracted to him and selfishly desiring him for myself.

After about three sessions with them he appeared at my office, alone. It was common for me to turn down walk-ins but I allowed him to cut into my schedule. He didn't waste any time explaining why he'd rudely showed up unexpectedly without an appointment. It seemed like none of that mattered to him. I tried to be aggressive, you know, play the professional role, but he had a plan that worked well in his favor in the end.

Rocky was the type that got what he wanted no matter how much of a challenge it panned out to be. I just happened to be one of the many he pursued…and conquered.

Before it was over, we were like two hungry animals on my floor, fighting to the death! He took possession of my body and locked me in a world that was filled with painful love. The more we had seen each other, the more foolish I had became. I had fallen in love with another woman's man.

After a few encounters, Amina made an appointment with me for another session. She didn't mention Rocky being present at this session so when he accompanied her, I was surprised. I would have thought he would have forewarned me. But, for his own egotistical reason, he felt there was no need.

I didn't like the vibe I was receiving from Amina as she took a seat on my lounger. I wanted to believe it was my own discomfort and not something she was suspecting between Rocky and I. I couldn't risk her finding out about us. Intimacy with a client was against the code of ethics. I would surely lose all I had if things had gotten out of control.

I was relieved to hear that I wasn't the topic after all. Amina just wanted to share how she felt Rocky was cheating on her and she needed my support on helping her through this. I sat there in awe, knowing I was the one to blame for the one causing the destruction of their relationship.

What made things even worse was the crazy faces he was making behind her back! I had to do everything in my power to pull myself together. I've asked myself many times why I didn't pick up then on how he loved to play with fire.

The more Amina went on, the deeper the session became. She revealed personal business of his that I could tell he didn't want exposed. Rocky became irritated and was ready to pick her up and haul her out. She made a comment on how she would die for him. She said something about moving bricks across the globe or something. At the time I didn't know what that meant. It wasn't until I became *his girl* before I found myself in that same position Amina was in. The only bad thing in all of the terrible things that happened in between was…I took the bullet…and she did the time…

A Drastic Encounter…
Amina & Monae

I learned the hard way that Amina wasn't going anywhere. She was more of an asset to Rocky. I had the choice of either dealing with her or suffering any consequences trying to leave the situation. I felt like I was stuck with the Mob or this was all some kind of sick set-up they both planned. Rocky had game like that, so it wouldn't have been hard to believe.

As time escaped us, Amina finally realized who the mystery woman was that invaded her space. This was one day I would never forget. I had just left Rocky, entering my office where she was impatiently waiting.

As I walked toward my secretary I didn't notice Amina sitting across from her. I tried to act normal, praying she hadn't seen me get out of Rocky's car. I was making excuses in my head just in case. Her presence was unexpected so I had to think fast. I could sense in her presence something was wrong, but I didn't want to believe that something was me.

"Hello, Amina. How are you?" I avoided eye contact.

Marilyn passed me some documents, so I used them to try and look busy. It gave me something to do rather than look her in the face.

"I guess I could be better. Yo, I need to talk to you Monae'. You got a minute?" Her speech was slurring. Rocky told me that she smoked at least an ounce of marijuana a day and on top of that popped pills! You would think that was more than enough to escape the reality of this world for good.

I wasn't getting a good vibe from her, but I couldn't afford for her to embarrass me. I approved the visit.

"Sure…follow me. Marilyn, hold all my calls, please." I threw a casual grin at my secretary then nodded for Amina to follow.

15

"Push that door up for me Amina, please. Thanks." I kept my head in the file in my hand. I was trying to hide the infamy of the whole situation.

"Have a seat." I placed the folder on my desk and turned to her, sitting on the edge.

"I'm not here for no damned counselin' session! I'm here for one thang and you know what the fuck it is!"

At any given moment I was expecting Marilyn to interrupt. She stood in attack position with an evil glare. I knew I had to play this, *I don't know what you're talking about* role to the bitter end. I had to do what I could to maintain a so-called conservative stance. My career was at stake with the presence of Amina. I had no choice but to do everything in my power to keep things mellow.

"Excuse me? I don't under...."

"BITCH! Let's get one thing straight!" She dropped her designer bag and started moving in closer. I watched the door praying for Marilyn to appear. "I ain't the muthafuckin' one! So don't try to play with my head! I had enough of that shit!"

She started pacing back and forth, massaging her temple.

Where's my back up when I need it?

My experience with flipping the script

16

didn't work with her at all. She wasn't trying to hear nothing I had to say.

"Look, Amina. Can we discuss this over lunch?" I attempted to talk over her loud and obnoxious voice. I tried to use all of my years of counseling skills and experience to calm her down.

"WHAT! LUNCH! Bitch please..." she laughed vindictively.

"Excuse me! I will not stand for this kind of talk Amina!" I attempted to take a defensive position.

"You better shut up and listen to what I have to say or it's going to be curtains up in this muthafucka! Now, where was I?" She was biting her nails. "Mph, I just want to understand something here Miss Psychologist! Rocky and I came to YOU for YOUR support and you gon' play me like this!"

I didn't know how to respond to this irate woman. My only position right then was to call security. I made an attempt to get to my phone and like a pit-bull breaking loose from his chain; it was over! Amina dived on me ripping my blouse from my body! Like a Damsel in Distress, I had to do all I could to defend myself. I attempted to reach for something to hit her with, but she was all over me like a lion in a jungle hungering for some flesh! It was the

fight of a lifetime! Frazier and Ali! We fought till
we both were tired. Hair was all over the place,
clothes were torn up, and still, no Marilyn....

Amina straightened herself up; acting like
nothing had happened then said,

"Now...this is the deal. You do you, and
I'll do me. I see you ain't know ho' when it
comes to the throw down. I like that in you Doc.
I know you're struck by the sudden change in
my attitude, but this is all a part of who I am. I
can't be replaced. Rocky and I are a package
deal. Take us...or leave us...you'll learn."

One thing she was right about...that was
the fact that I was struck by her change in
attitude. There I was, skin burning from
scratches she inflicted on me and she wants
me to act like nothing had just happened!

As I stood there observing her behavior
after our fight, I was able to determine that
Amina was a very disturbed woman. I felt after
this getting rid of her and having Rocky to
myself would have been easy, but again, I was
wrong. Rocky eventually controlled my
thinking, and my life! I was caught up with
Amina and several more before it was over. I
had fallen so deeply in love with him; the other
women and all of his manipulation and lies
didn't matter. I thought I couldn't breathe
without him and before I knew it I had become

his next employee.

None of that changed the fact that I was pushing for the number one spot. Everyday I found myself trying to move the rest of the women out of his life. I didn't realize that all of us were out to get each other. We argued and plotted against one another every second we got. Rock paid us no mind. I was beginning to think he liked watching us fight over him. That's when I took a new position. It was time for me to go to the next level.

A MAMA'S BOY...
Rocky

"ROCKY! Grab Isaiah for me!" Rocky's mom Sarah yelled down the stairs for him to get his baby brother off the potty-chair.

"You get 'um! I'm not about ta' wipe that lil' nigga's ass!" he responded.

Rocky was too into the bread he had flowing through a money counter to tend to any of his mother's needs right then. When it came to his stash he trusted no one to keep track of it but him. That was his number one rule in the game that he knew very well.

"I refuse to let you piss me off this morning, Rocky!" Sarah yelled coming through the kitchen with little Isaiah on her hip. "You could have got this boy for me!"

She placed Isaiah onto the floor and walked over to the cabinet to grab something for the baby to eat.

"I didn't have'um. What I look like changin' a diaper? If I wanted the headache, I would knock one of my girls up. Come here little man. Let cho' big bro show you somethin'." He reached out for Isaiah, picking him up, placing him on his lap. "No. Don't put that in your mouth." Rocky had to pry bills from the baby's hands. He placed a peck on his cheek and sat him back on the floor.

"Ma, you need anything before I pack up?"

"Umm, I'm okay. Take care of yourself son. But I will say this; the next time I tell you to do something...."

"Gon' somewhere with that." he waved her off as he placed stacks of bills in rubber bands and dropped them into a bag.

"Booooy...don't make me..." she walked over and playfully raised her hand to him. He laughed at her and continued to work with his dough. Even little Isaiah thought it was funny.

He loved his mother more than life itself. She wanted for nothing. There was nothing he wouldn't do for her. He could be a little too overprotective at times and that got on her nerves. But she realized what her son had been through and, that alone, granted him a lot of control over her decision-making. It could be complicated at times because she had to hide her relationships from him to avoid his ignorance. But overall, he was her love and her heart. He was a 'Mama's Boy'.

The Hood Hall of Fame...
Rocky

Rocky had been the man of the house ever since the death of his father, Larry. Larry had no respect for his son, Rocky, or Rocky's mother, Sarah. He would come home angry over something one of his other women had done and would commence to beating on Sarah to release his tension. Rocky grew tried of picking his mom up off the floor, covered with blood and bruises. He loved Sarah too much to see her go through abuse by a candy-snorting-bootleg pimp. That was what Rocky named him after witnessing him use drugs several times. Rocky knew that if he didn't do something soon, Sarah was sure to die.

Larry's only employment outside of pimping was selling drugs. Every dime Sarah received from him went straight to the welfare of her son. Larry was far from a father to Rocky and that ruined any chance of a father-son bond ever being established. Sarah knew if she didn't find a way out, something bad was going to happen.

Rocky was able to do without the love from his sperm donor, so he made the streets his father. He knew more about his hood than the average child when he was just nine.

Rocky learned a lot from the men he hung out with. They schooled him on everything a young player should know. He had the aim of a sharp shooter and game like TuPac. Every one used to tell him he reminded them of the late TuPac Shakur. He would just smile and accept it as a compliment. Though Rocky was never a follower he made an impact on his neighborhood the day his father was killed. That gave him a signature on the Hood Hall of Fame. He's been respected ever since.

Rocky purposely stayed out late to avoid his parent's issues. When he came in every night he feared finding Sarah dead. She was so caught up in her own nightmare; Rocky's late-night whereabouts never crossed her mind. She felt by not enforcing a curfew on him was the only thing she could offer him for the time being.

One late night Rocky came home and heard Sarah screaming for her life! He stormed through the front door to find his father in the kitchen twisting his mother's arm behind

her back to the breaking point! Sarah's eyes
were red and Rocky could literally feel her pain.
Instantly he grabbed Larry's arm and attempted
to pull him off his mother. Larry slung him,
slamming his small frame against the wall.
Larry was so high off of cocaine that he turned
into a monster. Suddenly he pulled out his gun,
and pointed it at Rocky! Sarah screamed,
"DON'T HURT MY BABY!"

It was then that Larry backhanded Sarah
and knocked her to the floor. Rocky wanted to
make an attempt to snatch the gun from his
hand but Larry was 6'6.

He used his head and walked away. The
only thing going through his mind was, the
same man that lay up with his mother to create
him, was the same one that was ready to take
his life. Rocky knew right then he had to make
a decision that would transform their lives
eternally.

He sat in his room contemplating. He
was startled by a door slamming. When he
peeped out he noticed it was Sarah's bedroom
door. Rocky stepped out of his room, walked
toward the living room area, and noticed Larry
standing by the window snorting cocaine. Larry
didn't see Rocky standing behind him holding
the gun that he had carelessly left on the
counter. It wasn't until Rocky cocked the gun

that Larry realized his life was in the hands of an angry and very bitter nine year old gangster. Larry turned around dropping some of the nose candy to the floor, stunned.

"You little' muthafucka! Give me that damned gun!" Larry reached out.
Rocky rose the gun aiming it at Larry's head and within seconds, he unloaded, Larry crumpled to the floor.

"Rest in peace muthafucka...." Rocky dropped the gun and walked out the front door. The only thing he heard were Sarah's screams as he disappeared in the darkness.

Sarah was shook up over the incident. The last thing she wanted was for her son to get charged with killing his father. Her first reaction was to make it look like she was the one responsible when the police got there. Her plan backfired and Rocky was taken into custody.

It was the grace of God that saved her son. Not only weren't there any laws that charged minors as adults at the time; but the fact that their neighbors were able to testify in court about the abuse that Sarah and Rocky had suffered from over the years helped to reduce the charges to self-defense of a minor.

Rocky was reborn. From pushing large quantities of cocaine, to dominating his neighborhood, he was one of Detroit's largest drug dealers. Sarah didn't necessarily condone the behavior but Rocky was the decision maker and breadwinner in the home. Sarah was left to depend on him to take care of her. She loved her son either way. Not to exclude the fact that she was reaping in large benefits and living a lavish lifestyle. He set her up with her own Deli and Car Wash and she loved and lived it up.

Rocky gave her the world. From the outside looking in you would have thought Sarah was the one holding the cash and selling the drugs. That's what lured Paul in. His only objective was to take control over what he thought was hers. Sarah didn't tell Paul right off about her son and Paul wasn't upfront about his son, Kenneth.

They both had their own selfish reasons but, Sarah more than Paul had to be careful as far as she knew then. Telling her male acquaintances in the past about Rocky didn't do anything but run them away. Rocky's reputation for killing his father scared them and that was that. She didn't want to risk that with Paul. Sarah was attracted to him and she wanted to wait until the time was right to introduce him to Rocky. But after Paul purposely got her pregnant she had no other choice but to tell her son about her new friend. Rocky freaked out. He didn't speak to Sarah through half of her pregnancy.

Paul hated Rocky and the fact that he controlled the cash register. But he felt the closer he had become with Sarah, the more control he would gain over the money she had stored in her possession.

Three months before Sarah had their child Paul proposed and she accepted. Before Sarah moved forward on her wedding plans she made an attempt to get through to Rocky. She told him that he couldn't run her life and that she needed to make her own decisions. She informed him that she didn't need to ask him for permission. "Let me be me Rocky. I love you and no man can ever take that away."

Rocky stepped aside, not because he had to, but because he respected Sarah and her decision. None of that changed the fact that he didn't care for Paul. And in his own words he told him if he was to ever disrespect his mom in any way, he wouldn't hesitate. If he could kill his father… placing another bullet through another man's heart was simple. Paul wasn't moved by that. It only made it easier to move forward with his plan.

Sarah was pleased to have both Paul and Rocky back in her life. A family was something she had always dreamed of having. But in the end, what was set out as a dream turned into a nightmare… Sarah would have never expected Paul would have stripped her from someone more precious than life.

Less of a Man…
Paul

Paul entered the kitchen yawning after getting out of bed.

"Hey Rocky, hey Bay." He spoke to both of them and kissed Sarah on her forehead. Rocky nodded.

"Come here daddy's man!" he said as he swooped up Isaiah into his arms.

"You want me to fix you something to eat before you head out?" Sarah asked Paul, grabbing a carton of eggs out of the fridge.

"That nigga' ain't got know slave up in here. He can cook his own damned eggs." Rocky rudely intercepted.

"You better keep bagging that money, boy." She snapped.

"It's okay Sarah." Paul said. "I'm alright." He passed Isaiah to her. "I need to get out of here and head over to the car wash." He grimmed Rocky.

Paul knew he wasn't going to be able to take much more of Rocky. He had this way of making him feel like he was less of a man. If it wasn't for Paul impregnating Sarah, the whole marriage would have never taken place.

In due time muthafucka, in due time. Soon the ball will be in my court, Paul silently said to Rocky as he left the kitchen.

Rocky knew it was time for him to hit the streets. Sarah was going off on him for the way he talked down to Paul, so he made his way out the door. He couldn't help the way he felt about the whole situation. The more Rocky looked at Sarah and Paul the more irritated he became. He tried to work with his personal issues toward Paul, but ever since Paul's son, Kenneth, came in the picture, the acceptance process had gotten worse. Rocky didn't have any tolerance for Kenneth. He called him artificial and wanted no parts of him! But Sarah, with the Rodney King quote: *"Can't We All Just Get Along?"* forced him to give Kenneth a chance.

Keep Your Enemies Close
Amina & Monae'

"I know you don' heard." Amina said annoying the hell out of me with her gum smacking and blowing bubbles.

"Heard what?" I exhaled, rolling my eyes

up in the air trying to ignore her. I was frustrated with this whole last minute layout Rocky placed together. Amina found it easy to aggravate me and I wasn't in the mood to hear what was about to come out of her mouth. She was always intentionally trying to piss me off.

"Oh, so you don't know. I thought you and Rocky shared everything." She sarcastically commented.

"Look Amina, we have a long day ahead us and I don't feel like getting into it with you right now. I'm tired and I need to get some sleep before this plane lands. So whatever it is you got to say...say it." I turned my head in the other direction.

"You a trip, Monae'. But I'm gon' let you have that attitude. I just wanted to know did you hear about the baby." I looked at her with an attitude saying to myself, *Bitch! You better not be pregnant by Rocky!*

"Don't look at me like that! I'm not the one that's knocked up, Boo! It's the new comer, Erikah..." She gave me a devilish grin.

"BY WHO?" People were starting to stare at us 'cause I was so loud.

"Yo boy, yo man, the love of your life...."

"Fuck you, Amina. You tryna' start some shit!"

"Whatever, ask her, you'll see." She

turned over like she was about to go to sleep.

There I was tolerating his ex on a plane. handling business for him, and he was out there making babies by some other chick! If Amina wasn't lying, I had every intension of leaving him after that! Quiet as kept, I should have tossed them drugs we were picking up in a near by river and left Amina to have to explain. I was risking my life for him and he had the nerve to do me that way. Not to mention all the drugs I had smuggled for him before this unexpected run with his crazy ex!

Was I that damned naive?

When we made it to Miami, I had an attitude and thought back on a lot of shit. Amina loved every moment of it, too. She had been trying everything in her power to get me out of the picture. She stayed in competition with me ever since the office fight. I ended up losing my practice over that! I have to give it to Rocky though. He was smooth in the way he brought Amina and me together. I even allowed him to talk me in to allowing her to sleep with us!

The more I thought about all the things I had done for him out of love, the more foolish and dirty I felt. I found myself being pulled deeper into his trap. Never once had he apologized for any of the pain he caused me.

Yet I was still there to do what ever he asked of me.

We took a cab to the hotel and once we made it there the only thing I wanted to do was lie down and cry.

"So what do you wanna do, Monae'? Are we gon' get separate rooms? Or do you want to get one together." Amina gave me a devious grin. I stood at the front desk preparing to pay for our rooms with my VISA, ignoring her.

"Do you have a reservation Ma'am?" the desk clerk asked.

"Yes sir. My name is Monae' Moore. Could I please have an extra room? I stared at her and said, "Better luck next time honey." I didn't realize after saying that to her that I had spoken to soon.

"I'm sorry Ma'am, we're booked. But there are two beds in the room that you have reserved."

"That's fine, thank you."

"Damn, I was hoping it was only one bed for me and my girlfriend to share together." Amina teased, winking at the desk clerk. He had an embarrassed kind of expression on his face.

"That's not funny Amina. You can be so ignorant, I swear."

"Oooh, sweetheart...don't be like that."

I wanted to smack her so bad, but I knew I had to keep my cool. The man passed me my key along with a look of disgrace. I ignored him and made my way to our room. I wanted Amina to have her own room so badly! How unfortunate for me. How we both ended up here together was still a mystery. I was supposed to be on this run alone. Rocky said that the connect I was picking a package up from knew Amina personally. He felt her presence was necessary.

"Ai'ight, peep this. I'm supposed to meet this dude at 11 o'clock tonight. You can roll or you can stay. It doesn't make me no difference." Amina said changing into street clothes.

"I'll go. We came together, we roll together."

"Awwww shit! You startin' to talk like a real bitch now. Keep hangin' with me and I can show you some shit Boo!"

I just stared at her with a pitiful type expression on my face.

What were you thinking about when you got down with her, Rocky? The more I stared at Amina the more I was coming to my senses.

The rental car was delivered on time and it was time for us to handle business. I was feeling extremely nervous about this run.

Something just didn't sit right.

"You ready, bitch!"

"Amina...What I tell you about that bitch thang? I'm not one of them skanks you hang around. I wish you would stop, really."

"O'tay... Beeeuch! How does that sound Monae'? Is that better?"

"Let's get this over with Amina; so I can go home."

"Home is where the heart is..."

She threw the bag in the trunk and got in the car. We drove for almost an hour. I had to listen to rap music the whole time. Somebody called a *T.I.* she was playing had my head pounding! It was driving me nuts, but it kept her from bothering me, so I tolerated it. She obviously knew where she was going and the closer we got the worse it felt. This old neighborhood was trashed. It was a run down neighborhood that you only see in scary movies. It was dark and I was really very uncomfortable. Rocky made the right decision when he sent Amina. There would have been no way I would have conducted any type of business in a neighborhood like this.

"Where the hell are we going, Amina?"

"Just shut up and drive."

"I'm going to let you have that one."

"You don't have a choice. Pull over there

behind that guy in the Marauder."

"I know you don't think I'm going to park in this dark alley to do no transaction!"

"You finish?"

She gave me this look that challenged my life with hers. I felt like we both had guns and may the best girl live.

I pulled behind the car and silently started to pray. There was a part of me that felt God was somewhere else at the time and I was on my own.

"Pop the trunk." She jumped out and walked around the back of the car to retrieve what I was told was money. The guy in front of us never turned back. A part of me wanted to see his face, but he never gave me that satisfaction. It was like I was sitting in the middle of Camp Crystal Lake waiting for Jason.

"Hold tight Ma! I'll be back to kiss that pussy again in a minute," she challenged.
I was so nervous. I was still sensing something was about to happen. I just ignored her stupid comment.

She knocked on the guy's window and he let her in. I was able to see some movement between the two of them. Whatever he was saying, she seemed aggravated. Then out of the blue, his fist hit the dash! Something wasn't right! My heart was skipping beats, and

I was seriously thinking about pulling off and leaving her. I was squenching my eyes trying to make out what was happening. Then, Amina lost it! I could see her pointing in his face, expressing disappointment! They were arguing back and forth. My first reaction was to blow the horn, but before I could bring myself to that blood splattered across the back window. I froze! I felt paralyzed, not knowing what to do next!

"MONAE'! SNAP! OUT OF IT! PULL THE FUCK OFF!" I shouted out loud to myself! I lost control! Before I could drop the car in gear, Amina jumped out of the other car with two bags; one in her hand and the other clutched under her arm. She was racing in my direction. It took a minute before I noticed the chrome reflection against my headlights coming from her hand! That's when I knew that it wasn't her blood that was streamed across the guy's car... it was his! This crazy broad blew the guy's head off! The last thing I wanted to do was to let her back inside the car! My first mind told me to pull off!

"MONAE', I WILL SMOKE YO'ASS, IF YOU DON'T STOP THE MUTHAFUCKIN CAR AND UNLOCK THIS DAMNED DOOR!"

I knew she meant every word and I felt obligated. It was all a set up and that night I was going to die. Her day had finally come to get me out of the picture.

Once she got inside, she told me to pull off! I never once questioned her about what happened.

"Look at cho' scary ass!" she giggled, wiping blood from her hands. She laid the gun on the floor, opened the bag that had the drugs packed inside. "HELL YEAH!" she said in a high-pitched tone.

I didn't get it. She had just blew someone's head off and she's clicking her heals?

"You ai'ight?"

"No you didn't just ask me that, Amina." I was so nervous, I couldn't even cry.

"See, that's why I don't understand why Rocky don't put you up on shit. You know I ain't the one who planned this, Monae'. Your man you connived to steal from me did it. I'm just following orders. That's all." she smiled, deviously.

Now I really felt sick. I was set up to go on a robbery with *La Femme*, the assassin! Rocky had taken this too far! He and his women are nuts! Amina and Rocky had this hit all mapped out. She had brought her an extra pair of clothing to change into and had our tickets ready for us to jump on a flight right afterwards! We went by the hotel to grab our things and that was the last time I would ever see Amina or Miami!

Should I Leave or Should I Stay?
Monae' & Rocky

"You still mad at me?" Rocky asked me while I was typing some paper work on a building to start up my own business.

"No Rocky. I allowed you to do this to me. I can't be upset with you for making that choice." I continued working on my computer.

"Listen. Stop typing for a minute and look at me," he demanded as he turned my chair around to face him. "I have a lot of things going on in my life at this time, Monae'. You know that. This thing I do here is business. I know I didn't tell you about Amina's job, but you were able to see it for yourself." I stared away at the monitor.

"Rocky, I trusted you. I've been placing my life on the line for you out of love! Does that sound crazy to you, because it damn sure sounds crazy to me! You placed me at risk and sent me on a job without informing me what was going on. That sounds pretty fucked up for a person in love to do for her man. Or better yet, what kind of man that loved his woman would use her that way? This is not about love.

This is about you! How could you use me like that Rocky? I thought we were better than that! Why?" I cried.

My father used to tell me not to ever let a man see you cry. There was something about the tears that gave a man all the control to fuck over you even more.

"Baby, I know that you're upset right now and I know there is very little I can say that would change what has already happened. But you need to know that if I didn't get that nigga first, he would have gotten me. Is that what you want? I couldn't let that happen, Monae'." He pushed. He was good at making excuses, but even they were growing old. I realized at that point if I stayed with Rocky it wouldn't have been long before I became a drug lord's suicide bomber! He continued to mislead me with his lies and manipulation.

"Are you listening to me Monae'?"

"I hear you, Rocky. And to answer your question…no, I don't want anything to happen to you. But that's not the only thing you have done that I feel is serious. What about Erikah….?" I looked into his eyes searching for an explanation.

"I don't know what you're talking about. What do you mean, what about Erikah?"

He placed his defense shield up. He

doesn't like it when he was placed on the spot about something. It makes him angry. That's how I could tell when he was lying…he would become annoyed.

"Oh, so you weren't going to share the good news? The baby, Rocky! What's up with that?" I was vexed!

"I'm not going to get into that with you right now, Monae'. Let's talk about something else." He looked away, messing with the keyboard on the desk.

"Oh, you gon' play me like that, huh? Oookay. I knew it would come to this, so I made sure I was prepared. I'm moving into my own place. I can't take this anymore."
I rose out of the chair and started walking toward the bedroom.

"You do whatever makes you happy. If moving into yo' own shit makes you happy, do you." He walked off and went down the hall somewhere.

I couldn't believe he didn't try to stop me. That's what hurt the most. I had it already made up in my mind it was time to go, but there was a part of me that wanted him to beg me to stay.

The apartment I leased was nice. I had saved up every dime he'd ever given me. Plus I had money of my own saved for a rainy day. I wasn't a big fool like the rest of them targets he messed with. Their only interest was to see who could afford the most expensive outfit or sport the largest diamond. I didn't care about all of that material stuff. I just wanted to be loved.

A New Start...I Thought
Monae'

It had been a couple of weeks since I'd heard from Rocky. I missed him and came close to calling him several times. I knew I had to be strong if I didn't want to spend the rest of my life being unhappy. In an effort to keep my mind off of him I purchased a building in Southfield to start up a counseling program for teens suffering from HIV. I felt the need to turn my attention toward those who truly warranted my professional attention. It helped me to place my thoughts elsewhere, for the time being.

Never Let a Woman See You Sweat
Rocky

I knew that I wasn't shit when it came to women. I've come to realize that. I shouldn't have been this way after all my mother had been through. I've tried to ignore the fact that my father wasn't shit. But I've inherited a lot of his ways. I sold drugs and have done a little pimpin' here and there. I love control and all kinds of pussy; loose pussy, tight pussy, smelly pussy, I just love me some pussy! And that's why I can't see myself locked down with one woman. I could never see myself workin' no 9 to 5! That's how the white man got it set up! I hated going to school and I had no intention of going to college. That shit ain't for black people! They teach us to become slaves! To work for the white man instead of teaching us to own some shit! Fuck that! Selling drugs may be fucked up, but it's all I know and I'm good at it. I ain't worried about no FEDS and no nigga' out here on the streets killin' my ass! I'm one step ahead of the game and I'm ready to die to get mines! I'm a soldier...

Okay...now let me be serious. I think I love that damned Monae'. I ain't never had no woman leave me like she did. I miss her and I have to admit it. My pride won't allow me to call her, but I may have to break down 'cause I'm missin' that ho for real.

Slipped
Monae'

Never say never was all I could say to myself. Rocky had been staying at my place off and on now. He called me and I was so happy to hear from him. Nobody, again, could've told me something would ever go wrong between us. We went from; how have you been doing to; I'm on my way over there, and it's been on ever since. The distance did something to us. Maybe it was something we needed to happen between us. Things may have just been moving too fast in the beginning, I don't know. I was just glad he broke down and called me first. I felt superior for holding out the longest.

He was happy to hear how my business had grown and how I was slowly getting my life together. I was becoming comfortable with being alone, but I didn't tell him that. I had fallen in love all over again. He had me wrapped around his finger so tight I was sure to fall victim to him again. It was like my feelings were stronger than the time we first met. That alone was dangerous. Decisions...

A Fugitive of Foolish Love
Monae' & Erikah

"Hello?"

"Monae'...this is Erikah. What time are you picking me up?" She asked, breathing kind of hard in phone.

It was about four in the afternoon and I had just made it in from the office. Rocky wanted me to take her on one of her prenatal visits. Her appointment wasn't until 5:30 so I really didn't understand the purpose of her call.

"I thought we'd already discussed this, Erikah," I yawned.

"I-I...I know, Monae'. I was just gon' make a quick run, but I'll be back by the time you get here. I've been trying to call you for the last hour."

"What's wrong with you? Is the baby okay? Why are you breathing like that?"

"Girl, you know I'm seven months now. Hell, this baby is about to take me off my feet. I'm tired."

"Alright, let's see...I will be leaving my place in about another 15 minutes."

"Good. That'll work. Bye."

There I was again, caught up in Rocky's love triangle. First I was moving his dope now I'm transporting his tribe. I'm better off dead than to be going through this bullshit with this fool.

And Pregnant Pussy...I left that out...
Rocky

"What she say...she comin'?" Rocky moaned while Erikah was straddling on top of him.

"SSSMMMM....yessss baby....sh-sh-she

said she will be here in about f-fifteen minutes….uuuuhhhssss," she moaned. Erikah was another one that wanted Rocky all to herself. Having a baby was one of the many things she had in store for him.

"That's daddy's little girl in there. You see how greedy yo' mommy is?" Rocky teased her as she continued to ride him like it was her last time. She was getting hers, big bellied and all. None of that got in the way of her receiving a nut.

"Sssmmm…you love me Rocky?" She moaned as she rode him slow finding that hot spot that made her body quiver.

As she fell deep into her rhythm, she cupped both of her baby-swelled breasts in her hands, draping her tongue across her nipples. Rocky held on to her waist laughing to himself as she reminded him of this possessed chick from a movie they watched earlier on bootleg. Her eyes were rolling around and she had strands of saliva streaming down on his chest. He just wanted her to get hers so he could chop it up and roll out.

"So you not gon' answer my question, huh?" Erikah continued.

Rocky was willing to tell her anything she wanted to hear at that time. Concentrating more on the feeling of the pregnant womb made it even easier to get his and fill her head with a little pillow talk. But more importantly, he knew he had to get ghost before Monae' pulled up.

Monae'

"How did things go with the doctor today with Erikah?" he asked lying, on his side with his back turned while I was reading a book.

"That's your baby mama. Why you didn't call and ask her?" I was irritated.

It's bad enough that I belittled myself by having anything to do with this child he had knocked up, but I'm trying to be down for my man, so I had to calm down.

"My bad." He brushed off my attitude. "Scratch my back baby."

"I guess I'm good for something." I sat my book on the stand. "Scratch it where Rocky?"

"Right there, Bay." He guided me to the spot.

"It looks like somebody beat me to it." I noticed something that appeared to be scratches.

"Cut it out Monae'."

"Anyway, the doctor said she and the baby looked pretty healthy." I didn't want to take them marks to another level. I guess I finally accepted the fact that I have a ho' for a man.

"Wake me up at six. I got some business to take care of. By the way Monae', I need you to handle something for me. I'll leave you a note of instructions under the pillow. I already got it laid out. I left it in my car. I'll get it in the morning."

"As long as it's not a hit, we're in business," I said thinking about crazy Amina.

"Yeah...okay."

There was a part of me that wanted to cry when he showed concern about Erikah and their baby. Not only did he carelessly ask me about her day at the doctor, he never once apologized about the baby, her, or anything he's ever taken me through! Then to make it even worst, he's placed me back in business. The only thing he has ever written down for me in the past was how to get to a place where a transaction was going down.

Lord, please help me to wake up from this nightmare.

Laying Out the Plan...
Paul & Kenneth

"The bitch wouldn't budge, Kenneth!" Paul angrily expressed to his son sitting in Kenneth's rundown home in Inkster. "I don't know why in the hell I wasted my time marrying that ugly ho'! I should've known not to go after her money with that crazy son of hers in the way!" He finished up his drink and tossed it to the ground next to all the other trash.

"Well...like I suggested before; you just gon' have to do what I said at first. Get rid of the muthafucka! He's in the way Paul! Ain't no sense in trying to get a dime out of that ho', 'cause she ain't givin' up shit as long as Rocky's running it," Kenneth confirmed.

"I know one thang. If I don't get my hands on some cash in another week, I'm dead. You know Reggie and his people don't play around about their shit Kenneth," he said impatiently. Paul was becoming frustrated with a yellow jack that was flying around him. "I hate bees!" He tried to duck and wave the angry bee away.

"It's that expensive shit you wearing! You see it ain't fuckin' with me." Kenneth laughed.

"I wouldn't fuck with you neither! You the only nigga I know that believe in placing deodorant over funk and you wonder why you by yourself!" Paul said as he killed the bee in his hand.

"I'm gon' ignore that and write it off as a father's way of showing his love to a son he never claimed."
Paul just stared at him and flicked, the bee in

the air, and continued their conversation.

"Like I was saying. I got to get my hands on the bread, son.

"Oh…I'm *son,* now." Kenneth looked surprised. He'd never heard Paul call him son.

"Be serious Kenneth."

"That's better Pops."

"I'm going to ignore this tit-for-tat. Now, as I was saying, *Kenneth*…I can't let no around the way thug take me out over some old shit. The debt has to be paid no matter what it costs."

"Well I guess our meeting is done here. And for what it's worth, I ain't gon' let nobody fuck with you, Paul! I'll kill'a nigga first!"

"Well that finalizes everything. You kill Rocky and all our problems will be over. I kind of feel sorry in a way though."

"What you mean?" Kenneth asked hawking and spitting on the grass.

"I have a son by this ho', Kenneth. At first I didn't give a fuck about the leach! Now he's kind'a grown on me." He said in deep thought. "I don't know Kenneth. Maybe I should reconsider this whole set up," he contemplated.

"Com'on Paul! You and I both know that you don't have a fatherly bone in yo' body! If you would of said anything else I may have taken it into consideration, but having sympathy for that baby, hell naw! You didn't give a fuck about me so why be daddy now!"

Kenneth was becoming irritated and he was trying to hold back all his years of pain without his father. Recapturing the past was starting to set off a rage that made him want to take this whole thing to another level. If it had been up to Kenneth, he would have the blood of a two year old on his hands with no remorse.

Paul sensed the disturbance in his tone and immediately used the gift of reverse psychology. "I guess you're right Kenneth." Paul threw his hand on Kenneth's shoulder to snap him out of his gaze. Kenneth sprung back to pick up where they left off.

"Think about it this way Paul. Once Rocky is out of the way, Sarah will be so distraught, she won't even know what hit her," he said persuasively. "I've been watching that bitch Monae' real close and I know her every move. I'm willing to bet she holds his loot up in that fancy condo she got downtown off the river front."

"You probably right Kenneth. I never thought about that. That girl is always around him too! That's got to be where he hides the money. What you know about that other girl he was about to marry before this new one came around?"

"That Lil' Kim knock off from the hood?
You talkin' about Amina. Bitch was crazy as
fuck too. I heard she was layin' niggas down for
that fool."

"I'm impressed. You know now that I think
about it, she's the one Sarah was talking on the
phone about to her sister. That girl just got six
years for trafficking drugs through Georgia."

"Who shit was it, Rocky's?"

"Of course. I was hoping the Feds got
him before I did, but she wouldn't tell on him.
She took a plea and laid it down for 6 years.
That boy must got some game son!"

"Naw, Paul. The bitch just stupid as hell. I
wouldn't of done a day for dude." Kenneth
smirked with vengeance and jealousy.

"Look at this here Paul. I got these
burnout chirp phones for us to communicate
back and forth. If you down, we could move on
this right away. With these phones, we can
cover our tracks. Neither one of us can afford
to get caught up."

"One thing I do know for sure is Rocky,
according to Sarah, has been staying out at the
new girl's place a lot." Paul said pressing
buttons on the phones.

"That big ass crib that nigga' got out there
in Birmingham and he staying in a small ass
condo with ole' girl?"

"I don't think he's living there. He's just over there with her a lot. That's why I believe the money I seen him counting in our kitchen is being stored at the chick's place. You know he doesn't leave it with his mom. Ever since I came into the picture, he doesn't trust leaving money in our home."

"Hmph. Well…you know they gon' have to die Paul." He stared at him vindictively.

"It is what it is…Son…"

Not Enough Hours in a Day…
Monae' & Rocky

"Ma! I'm getting ready to go to the crib! You need anything before I roll out?" Rocky yelled up the colonial staircase that he had designed to fit Sarah's luxurious home. Anything to please the only woman he truly loved.

"Yes! I do." She appeared at the top.

"Hurry up! I got some business to take care of!" he whined like the Mama's boy he was.

"Get your brother off his potty-chair," she smirked.

"And then you woke up…"
Rocky walked out the front door, jumped in his Benz and road off to his destination…

"Hi Daddy!"

51

"Hi Pumpkin! What did I do to deserve this call today?"

"I just wanted to check on you to see how you've been holding up. You work like a Hebrew slave. And it's not like you're an easy man to catch up with."

"I guess it is sometime possible that I over do things Monae'. I miss having you around me spending up all I've slaved for."

"Yeah, I bet. You know I won't hesitate to come over there and pocket a few duckettes." I laughed.

"What's mine is yours, Monae'. You're still my baby girl."

"You have to come over and see my new office when you get some time."

"New Office? Oh honey! You got the building! I'm proud of you! I never once said you couldn't do it Monae'. Wow." He proudly gestured.

"Yeah…things are starting to take off for me Daddy."

My mind drifted back to the phone call from Rocky. I couldn't get past what he wrote in them so-called instructions he left under the pillow! I know one thing…if he think I'm going to pick up ten Kilos or even one, he got me messed up in the game! I tore them instructions up as soon as he asked me that selfish question,

Did you take care of my business?
I found myself so caught up in my thoughts I
didn't hear my dad calling my name through the
earpiece.

"Daddy, I am so sorry. I lost you for a
minute." I lied.

"Are you okay Pumpkin?" He sounded
concerned.

"No. I mean yes! Yes Daddy, I'm fine!
And not only am I well, my business is doing
well and I want you to see what I've done!"
I shut him out once again. We used to be able
to talk about anything, but now I have too
much pride to admit to him that he was right
and I was wrong.

"What are your plans for tomorrow
Pumpkin?"

"You are my plans Daddy. I miss you and
I would really like to see you."

"How does 5:30 look on your schedule?"
He was excited.

"I will be right here waiting for you
Daddy."

"I'll call tomorrow and get the directions
before I leave. I love you Pumpkin."

"I love you too, Daddy." I hung up the
phone and shut everything down. I had my
mind made up that when I met up with Rocky at

my place, there wouldn't be no movie and no more trips to the doctor with his tramp! I want my keys and it's over between us, I mean it this time.

Never Had the Chance to Say Goodbye
Never Had the Chance to Change...

"POP! POP! POP!"
Kenneth shot Rocky in his chest forcing the weak wood on the chair to collapse. I was so traumatized I passed out!

When I woke up, it was only for a moment. There were several doctors standing over me and my head was spinning! I could hear voices that sounded distorted and loud! My eyes were burning from the bright light that was shining from a big lamp above. I couldn't move or talk. I could hardly breathe! Something that felt like needles were pinching me all over my body! I found myself losing control and trying to keep my eyes open.

The Pain...The Loss...The Struggle...

Like any funeral, there were no words that could convey one's struggle with the loss of a loved one. Sarah hadn't been able to pull herself together since the day Monae's father, Orlando, found them both bound to chairs in her condo. The only person she had left that she trusted and confided in was Paul. He was able to put up a swell performance at the funeral. Sarah lost control when they made an attempt to close Rocky's casket. Paul did all he could to restrain her and prevent her from hurting herself in the process. Everyone mourned as the service went on, but what demonstrated how evil ones spirit could be was when Kenneth cried out, "THAT WAS MY BROTHER! WHY GOD? WHYYYYYY??"

Paul turned around, not only was he humiliated, but he was uncomfortable not knowing what others were possibly thinking. He felt exposed after Kenneth's imprudent approach. Paul tuned out all the negative vibes he was feeling and continued to console his wife.

Anticipation

Seven days after the funeral and Sarah was still a walking zombie. Many of the relatives that attended the funeral were still in town. Their presence came in handy when it came to helping with Isaiah. It was greatly appreciated. She spent most of her time at the hospital with Monae', still in a coma.

Paul has been following Monae's progress closely. He knew the consequences he and Kenneth would have to face if she awoke from her coma. Though Paul had himself to blame for only assuming she was dead. He knew he had to move forward with plan B... kill anyone who stepped in his way.

Sarah sat in a chair next to Orlando and they both watched her chest rise up and down with the assistance of a respirator. With very little said to each other, the only other person to seek help from at that point was God.

An Unexpected Guest

"Oh my God, Kenneth, you scared me." Sarah nervously said.

Monae's father had just left a couple of hours ago to go home and shower. Sarah didn't want to take a chance of not being around if she had awakened so she showered at the hospital.

"Sorry about that. How's my girl doing?" Kenneth asked as he surveyed Monae's room.

"The same." Sarah stared over the head of the chair at Kenneth. "What are you doing here? Paul told me you were out of town for the weekend." She was a bit confused. She got up out of the chair and walked over to Monae' and rubbed her forehead as tears welled up in her eyes.

You poor soul... she consoled silently.

"I feel so sorry for her, Sarah. She's

suffering so badly. And I really hate what all of this has done to you and Paul." Kenneth said, taking a seat in Sarah's chair.

"Thank you, Kenneth." Sarah reached to give his hand a firm squeeze. "Do you mind watching over her while I go and grab me something to eat from the cafeteria? I haven't had much of an appetite since this has happened."

"My pleasure Sarah." *I thought you would never ask,* he said to himself.

"Thanks." She grabbed up a few of her belongings, looked over at Monae', and made her way out of the room. Kenneth made sure Sarah had taken off down the hall before he made his way over to Monae'.

"Hey little Mama, I see you fighting for your life."

The machines were starting to make additional noises. This hadn't happened since she fell into her coma. The sudden noise startled him. He felt uneasy and reacted quickly!

"When Paul shot you, I knew he didn't know shit about know damned gun! Now look at you, laying up in here like a vegetable," he whispered. "I heard you were pregnant by that dead nigga too! That shit is fucked up! Well..."

He sucked his teeth then continued,

"From the looks of things, you will all be together soon." He continued to whisper in her ear. "I know you're probably wondering to yourself, *how could a nigga be so cruel?* You will never understand baby girl." He lit a cigarette and ignored the "no smoking" sign. He prepared to make his move. He placed the cigarette out on the table and picked up the phone.

A Child Scorned...
Kenneth

Kenneth faced many bad experiences growing up. His mother was on drugs and his father, Paul, never gave a damn about him or his mother.

Paul shares the majority of the blame to the reason why Kenneth's mother turned out the way she did. Paul was very selfish and controlling back in them days.
Kenneth's mother depended on Paul to support them through the tough times, but he chose a different path that didn't include them.

Kenneth was one of those kids others his age teased and talked down to because of his clothing and hardly ever having his hair cut. That made growing up even more complicated for him. He was considered an outsider.
Kenneth thought when Paul had hit a lick he

would be able to fit in with his peers. None of that ever happened for Kenneth. Paul reaped all the benefits and threw it in their faces. He drove nice cars and carried beautiful women on his arm showing them no respect. Kenneth's mom would sometimes cry herself to sleep after hearing rumors of Paul spending money on other women and their children. Some days Kenneth wouldn't even have a clean pair of drawers or a decent pair of shoes to wear to school and when she would call Paul for help he would say, "You had him, you support him!"

From that point, she had selfishly convinced herself that the only way to escape the reality of her situation was drugs. She had help in making that decision by the company she kept. Before she knew it, the stars became her friend and life was no more.

Kenneth tried to reach out to Paul for help when he would see him in the streets. He would approach Paul, asking him for money to get food and some help for his mother. Paul would act like he didn't know Kenneth, treating him like he was a begging bum on the streets.

Kenneth's young eyes would cloud with tears as he stood there and watched Paul pull off with friends laughing and making jokes about the seed he planted. He had no understanding of how a human being could be so cruel.

Kenneth had to find strength, not only for himself, but also for his dying mother. Drugs were like acid to her soul. She was slowly deteriorating. Kenneth realized that there was no room left for change in Paul. Forced to accept the fact that he had a dead-beat dad, he decided to wield all of his energy in caring for his mother. He had to take on the man's role and try to run the household to the best of his ability. Kenneth struggled daily to keep food on the table and crack heads out of their home. Some days were even harder than others because at eight years old he was forced to become a man. Kenneth fought to take on all the responsibilities that a grown person had to, but his fight for survival had unexpectedly come to an end.

One day Kenneth was out hustling at different grocery stores, selling candy or anything he could to make a dollar. This day he had made over ten dollars and bought his mom home some of her favorite, Campbell's *Clam Chowder*. He always loved to see her smile through her yellow, stained, teeth when he would bring her something good. This had given him hope that she would have one day gotten better. To his regret, he found her dead on the bathroom floor from an overdose. Not only did finding her that way affect him mentally. It shattered every dream he may have possibly had in his life.

Several days passed before someone came by and found him lying next to her cold lifeless body. Because of the odor and the lack of any signs of consciousness they immediately called the police. Once Kenneth gained awareness, he screamed hysterically and lost focus of his surroundings. The police turned him over to the state because they were unable to contact any family members.

The officials were in the process of placing him into foster care when they located his father.

Paul had no intention of claiming custody of Kenneth. This was a man that showed no sadness due to the loss of Kenneth's mother. There was no way a man of his character would take any responsibility for raising a child. Without further adieu, he walked out of Kenneth's life leaving the authorities to do whatever they wanted with him.

There was a big part of Kenneth that hoped Paul would have sympathized with the situation and stepped up to the plate. But that small part that never believed in Paul won. Kenneth was placed into a circle of hell.

Kenneth shut down, not uttering word

from his lips. He lived with several families and was abused by the majority of them. It wasn't long before he started using his head and fighting back. He knew he had to survive or die in the process. He realized that he couldn't keep blaming himself for what happened to his mother. That was the reason he took so much abuse from his foster parents. It was his way of punishing himself.

Now, with a different outlook on his situation, he decided he would take the whole foster care thing to another level. He had to do whatever he could to reach his goal before his life was over. Kenneth only wanted to survive long enough to find the man who destroyed any mean of living. Finding Paul was his ultimate plan.

It wasn't easy for Kenneth to get out of the custody of the state. Even after what happened with the last two foster families, he still found himself sucked into the system. Due to the circumstances, Kenneth felt that the unexplained deaths that occurred while in care of the families would have been more than enough to let him go. He didn't want to accept that he was there for the long haul. Kenneth was still a minor during this time and the only one who made decisions over his life was the state. He came to the conclusion that the only way out of there was to escape.

In one of the homes he was placed in he thought the woman was possessed. She wasn't married and had temporary custody of him and two other children that were younger than him. She would tie the youngest child to a table to avoid her from moving around and getting into things. He would overhear the woman bragging to friends on how she would rather take care of children who couldn't talk. This was her way in ensuring they couldn't tell how they were being mistreated. She made an exception to her rule with Kenneth. He was strictly chosen out of greed and desperation. She needed more money and he was all the state had available at the time. The woman made his stay very uncomfortable. She tried to be discreet with how she was treating the other children because he could talk and tell, but she was able to find her way around that by blaming their bruises on him.

This made him angry. Kenneth thought back to all the other families that abused him when he was in his no-talking stage. He knew how those children felt and he had to do something before it was too late.

Kenneth didn't stay long under that woman's roof. An accident had taken place. The woman had taken things too far and

Kenneth became outraged. One night she beat the little four-year-old boy until he became hoarse. Kenneth thought the boy was dead because he could still hear the strap piercing the child's flesh and there was no screaming or crying. The woman once again blamed Kenneth for the child's bruises when the social worker came for a home visit. He was furious and realized it would be either him or her, so he got to her first. He placed some poison in her coffee one morning. He had gotten it from some junkie he saw on his way to school a few days before. This junkie used to use drugs with his mother and out of sympathy for Kenneth's loss, the guy got him what he needed to finish out his plan.

Kenneth knew the woman's routine so well that he knew exactly what to place the poison in and when. It took a few hours for the drug to react, but those hours were all he needed to make it worth his while. She went into cardiac arrest and they were off to another family.

It wasn't long after the woman's death before Kenneth was in the hands of another predator. This time things started off like a father and son bond but they ended up like a man that had a sick sexual desire for children. Twice this man raped Kenneth. This was simply two times too many. He knew he had to get out quickly or it would have been his life.

Killing the man came easy. One night he came into Kenneth's room assuming his position and out of nowhere Kenneth separated the man's penis from his body and left him to die. The social worker placed Kenneth in a psychiatric hospital for evaluation. That didn't last long before he had escaped. Now he was able move on to pursue his goal...bringing down Paul...

A Fallen Dream...

Kenneth burned a hole with his cigarette through the cheap wood on the table-stand next to Monae's bed. He pulled a silencer from under his shirt after he called the hospital security to Monae's room. He knew he had to work fast; not only because the guards were making their way toward the room, but more so because he knew Paul had located Rocky's stash and was counting the money at that very moment. Paul thought he had his pieces in order. He never once thought Kenneth had something in mind for him when it was all over.

Sarah heard Monae's room number being called out over the intercom. She immediately dropped her food than dashed toward the elevator! By the time she made it to the floor, they had it blocked off with staff, security and the Detroit Police! Sarah yelled for someone's attention saying, "THAT'S MY DAUGHTER IN-LAW!!! LET ME THROUGH!!!" She attempted to fight her way through the crowd, but it was useless.

"Who are you Ma'lm?" The officer grabbed her as she struggled to get loose.

"That's my daughter-in-law! What's going on? I have to get to her!" Sarah cried thinking the worst. She had no idea that the worst was yet to come....

Calling ALL Actresses and Actors With or Without Experience!!! CASTING CALL!!!!

Dear readers:

I am considering turning one of these stories into a Screen-Play, with your assistance. Please forward your favorite four stories to the address below, letting me know which one you feel should become a drama-filled Movie! I also ask that you leave your contact information being that I am seeking cast for four of the stories selected through your votes. This is my way in giving back to my audience who in fact made me who I am today.

Thank you for your support.

Valencia R. Williams

The Williams Sisters' Publication Group
P.O. Box 48541
Oak Park, MI 48237
Email: hottestsummerever@hotmail.com